BREE

Tomoko

Kenzie

Shelly

Jules

Camila

# THE DERBY DAREDEVILS

## Kenzie Kickstarts a Team

### BY KIT ROSEWATER

#### ILLUSTRATED BY
#### SOPHIE ESCABASSE

AMULET BOOKS
NEW YORK

Cataloging-in-Publication Data has been applied for and may be obtained from the Library of Congress.

ISBN 978-1-4197-4079-4

Amulet Books are available at special discounts when purchased in quantity for premiums and promotions as well as fundraising or educational use. Special editions can also be created to specification. For details, contact specialsales@abramsbooks.com or the address below.

Amulet Books® is a registered trademark of Harry N. Abrams, Inc.

**ABRAMS** The Art of Books
195 Broadway, New York, NY 10007
abramsbooks.com

For Brooke,
who brings out the daredevil in me . . .

and then watches while I run smack into walls
with my eyes closed.
—K.R.

# CHAPTER ONE

**"ROLLER DERBY PLAYERS, TO YOUR POSITIONS!"**

Kenzie Ellington snapped on her helmet and glided on one foot across the rink. Hundreds of KENZILLA banners rippled and waved in the crowd.

"Blockers at the ready!"

Shelly, Kenzie's best friend, cartwheeled onto the track and took her place next to Kenzie. The girls high-fived and crouched low. They balled their hands into tight fists.

"And—go!"

The referee blew a whistle, and the girls took off. They ducked and threaded past the other derby players in the pack. Their shoulders tapped as they skated side by side. The audience chanted their names.

*Zil-la! Zil-la! Bomb Shell! Bomb Shell!*

The jammer from the other team whipped around and came up on the girls fast. They nodded at each other. It was time for their special blocking move: the Crying Banshee.

"Ay yiiii!!!" they howled.

"Hold it!" someone called. The whistle blew again.

Kenzie blinked. The crowds and KENZILLA banners faded in her head. Suddenly she was back on the top row of bleachers, huddled next to Shelly.

"Uh-oh," Shelly whispered. "I think we were too loud again."

She pointed at the cluster of people staring up at them. A derby player on the track took out her mouth guard.

"Honey, are you OK?" the player asked.

Kenzie's cheeks reddened.

"I'm fine, Mom!" she called out.

The referee on the sidelines shook his head. "All right, ladies, another lap. Positions!"

Kenzie grumbled as she and Shelly stomped along the bleachers and took their seats next to Kenzie's dad and little sister, Verona.

"When do *we* get to skate?" Kenzie moaned.

"After your mom's practice ends," her dad said. "During Free Skate."

Kenzie shared a look with Shelly. They were not

interested in free skating. They were interested in *derby* skating.

The skating rink, along with the whole warehouse, belonged to Austin's roller derby league. Kenzie's mom had joined the league more than three years ago, when Kenzie and Shelly were still baby second graders. Kenzie wasn't allowed to participate in Free Skate back then, but now that she and Shelly were in fifth grade, they strapped on their skates every chance they got. Kenzie couldn't wait to turn fifteen so she could play in the derby "wreck" league, where teens got to train like real derby players until they joined the official teams. For now, she had to sit back and watch her mom and the other players knock each other around the track.

Verona poked Kenzie's side. "Why are you wearing a helmet?"

"For protection," Kenzie said.

"On the bleachers?" Verona asked.

Kenzie glared at her sister as she unbuckled the strap beneath her chin. Verona was only in kindergarten, but she sure loved to ask questions that made Kenzie feel like the younger sibling.

After three more rounds of the referee blowing the whistle and the derby players weaving past each other, Kenzie's

mom skated toward the girls. She plunked herself on the bleachers and reached for her water bottle.

"Nice blocking, Ms. E.," Shelly said.

"Thanks." Kenzie's mom wiped her face with a towel and took a long swig of water. "That new jammer on the Glitter Gals is amazing. Hey, Mambo!" She called a woman from the opposite team over. "Come meet my kids. Here's my oldest, Kenzie."

Kenzie waved at the tall, red-haired derby player standing in front of them.

"That's Verona by her dad," Kenzie's mom continued. "And this is Kenzie's friend Shelly."

Shelly smiled and nodded.

"Girls, this is Mambo Rambo."

Shelly's eyes went wide. "Is that your real name?"

"I wish," Mambo said, laughing. "It's my derby name."

"Mine is Kenzilla," Kenzie said.

"And I'm Bomb Shell," Shelly added.

"Ooh, I love both. So, when are you joining the Glitter Gals?"

"In a little less than two thousand days," Kenzie said. Not that she had been counting since third grade.

"Oh no you don't." Kenzie's mom wagged her finger at Mambo. "They'll be on the Hazel Nuts with me."

Mambo laughed again. "Well, I hope we see y'all on the track sooner rather than later," she said, her eyes glinting.

Kenzie grinned and reached inside the duffel bag for her skates. One day, derby teams really would be fighting over who would get her and Shelly. There had to be two spots, though. Shelly and Kenzie were a package deal. They had been the Dynamic Duo ever since their moms put them in the same Austin Tots daycare.

Kenzie stuffed her feet into her skates while Shelly went to the rental counter for her usual pair.

"Got the right ones?" Kenzie asked when Shelly came back.

"Yep," Shelly said. She tapped the spot of yellow paint on the back left wheel.

The girls sat shoulder to shoulder. They tugged hard on their laces and knotted them around their ankles, the same way they had seen real derby players do before rolling into practice.

The main warehouse doors opened, and a large group of families spilled in from the parking lot. Several boys whooped and hollered as they raced to the track. Kenzie sighed as she tightened her knee pads. It was hard to practice for derby during Free Skate. Most kids liked to go very fast in one direction, which was not so great when Kenzie and Shelly wanted to skate backward or turn together in circles for their Crying Banshee move.

"Come on," Kenzie said. She skated to the rink and carefully stepped one foot down, then the other.

"Hey, it's Bubble Girl!" one boy said, pointing at Kenzie's elbow pads and wrist guards.

"Try not to fall!" the boy next to him yelled.

Kenzie rolled her eyes.

"She wears them so she can fall and get back up," Shelly said. She tightened her helmet strap. "Unlike you two. You'd probably break your precious little bones."

Kenzilla and Bomb Shell glared until the two boys skulked away. Then they joined hands and slid onto the track. The girls took a few warm-up laps, racing each other around and around the loop.

"Let's work on some tricks!" Kenzie said, swiveling and skating backward.

They tried a few backspins. They tried hopping with both skates. They even tried skating with one leg in the air. But tricks were hard in roller derby, and both Kenzie and Shelly found themselves tumbling onto the ground again and again.

"You girls are fearless!" Mambo Rambo called. She flung her skates over one shoulder and gave a salute as she walked out the front doors.

Kenzie and Shelly beamed at each other.

"All right, ladies," Kenzie's dad called from the sidelines a while later. "Time's up. Kenzie, your mom needs a shower. Shelly, after a double sleepover, your mom probably needs a reminder of what you look like."

"Aw, come on, Dad," Kenzie said.

"We barely got started," Shelly added.

"Two hours ago!" Kenzie's dad cried. He signaled them

over. "Your toes are getting pruney from all that skate sweat. Bleachers! Sneakers! Let's go!"

Kenzie and Shelly shuffled their way off the track. Kenzie slid over to the front bleacher next to her mom, but Shelly kept skating toward the lockers.

"Bathroom," she said.

Kenzie nodded and sat down. She had only undone one of her laces when Shelly's face bobbed inches in front of her.

"That was a pretty fast bathroom trip," Kenzie said.

Shelly was breathless. "Forget about the bathroom. Come and see!"

She dragged Kenzie up by one arm. Their skates stumbled over the bumpy carpet until Shelly stopped at the giant bulletin board across from the bathrooms.

"Look!"

Kenzie squinted at the board. It was plastered with flyers.

"What is it? Tuba lessons? The free iguana?"

Shelly huffed and smacked her hand against a flyer in the center.

INTRODUCING

AUSTIN'S JUNIOR DERBY LEAGUE

GIRLS AGES 10–14

TRYOUTS SATURDAY, MARCH 1*

"That's only a week away!" Kenzie squealed.

She couldn't believe it. She and Shelly wouldn't have to wait two thousand days to play on the same team. They'd hardly have to wait seven days!

"Der-by time! Der-by time!" Shelly sang. She threw up her arms and wiggled like the inflatable tube dancers outside of car dealerships.

Kenzie laughed and read the poster again. A junior league that they could join. Kenzilla and Bomb Shell: the Dynamic Duo. It was almost too good to be true.

Then she noticed the tiny star next to the tryout date. A note in smaller letters was printed below.

*PLAYERS MUST TRY OUT INDIVIDUALLY.

COACHES WILL DETERMINE TEAMS.

"Oh no," Kenzie said.

Shelly stopped dancing. "What's wrong?"

Kenzie showed her the last line.

"We can't try out together."

# CHAPTER TWO

"IT'S NOT FAIR," KENZIE SAID THAT NIGHT OVER DINNER. "They shouldn't be allowed to separate the Dynamic Duo!"

"It's not really separating," her dad said. "You know how your mom's league practices. Even if you and Shelly do get put on different teams, you'll still be training together. Maybe you'll even scrimmage against each other."

Kenzie furrowed her brow.

She did not want to wave at Shelly across a rink. She didn't want to trade high fives at the very end of a game. Kenzie wanted to be a derby blocker on the track right next to Shelly, where they could look at each other and fly into their Duo formations at a moment's notice. They would be the talk of the league. All the other teams would have no idea what moves the girls had up their sleeves.

That was what playing *together* on derby meant.

"It's not the same," she said. She jammed her spoon into her mashed potatoes.

"Thanks, but the walls don't need to be replastered," her mom said, wiping up a splatter of potato that had landed behind her. "Maybe you'll get put on the same team."

"Maybe," Kenzie said. She brightened. "Maybe we'll both get put on a superstar team!"

"But don't you fall a lot?" Verona asked.

"You're supposed to fall in derby," Kenzie said. She stuck her tongue out at her little sister, but maybe, secretly, she was a little bit worried. Verona had a point. What if the other players at tryouts were really good and never fell, not even when doing tricks?

"Maybe you'll both get put on the easy team," Verona said. "For people who fall."

Kenzie growled and stuck her spoon back into the potatoes.

Her mom sighed and started collecting plates.

Kenzie's dad clasped his hands on the table. "Did I ever tell you about my bike-racing days?"

"Before or after?" Kenzie asked.

Kenzie liked to ask this question whenever her dad told stories about himself so she could imagine him more clearly. Since her dad was transgender, in some of his stories he looked more like a girl, and in other stories, he looked more like a boy. Actually, he was a boy all along, her dad had explained. But before he told people, they *thought* he was a girl. In his "before" stories, Kenzie's dad was like an undercover agent, with a secret only he knew. Kenzie wondered what it would be like to have a secret that big.

"After," her dad said, which meant when her dad wasn't keeping the big secret anymore, and everyone understood he was a boy.

"I used to race on my bike just before you were born. My

first team started out as complete newbies. We had never raced, and hardly knew each other."

"Uh-huh," Kenzie said. She could tell where this was going. Kenzie leaned away from the table. She found an oval in the ceiling plaster that looked like a derby track.

"But after we practiced together, we came in second at the Austin relay. Second! And you know who one of my teammates was?"

"Uh-huh." Kenzie imagined an invisible derby player twirling over the track. "Uncle Jake."

"That's right," her dad said. "He's one of our closest friends now. Maybe you'll make some new friends in derby . . ."

His voice trailed off as his eyes floated toward the ceiling. "What are you looking for up there?"

Kenzie blinked and looked across the table.

"A plan," she said.

"A plan for what?" her dad asked.

"For joining the league with Shelly."

Kenzie's mom turned off the faucet and dried her hands.

"Planning is better than whining," she said. "Let's come up with some ideas. Brainstorm!"

She fumbled around the junk drawer in the kitchen, then set down a piece of paper and the stub of a purple crayon in front of Kenzie. "Maybe you can think of some ways to keep the Dynamic Duo together."

Kenzie stared at the paper. It seemed so big and so blank. How was she supposed to fill it up with ideas?

"My brain isn't stormy enough," she said, slumping over the table. She closed her eyes. "I wish I could be in charge of making the teams."

"Hang on," her mom said. "That's not a bad idea."

"What isn't?" Kenzie asked. She sat up again.

Her mom tapped her chin. "Let me call the Hazel Nuts coach. Maybe she'll know more about the junior league."

Kenzie's mom grabbed her phone and went into the living room of their apartment. Kenzie waited a moment, then ducked under the table and snuck in after her. She crawled

on her belly until she was behind the couch. Her mom sat with the phone already pressed tight to her ear.

"Right. Yes. That does make sense. Very fair. OK—thank you, I'll let her know!"

The phone clicked. Kenzie popped up behind her mom.

"Can they put me and Shelly on the same team?"

"It's a tryout," her mom said. "I can't ask the officials to put you on a team already."

Kenzie frowned. "What did your coach say?"

"She said she has to double-check with the league head, but she thinks a group can try out together."

"Yes!" Kenzie said. She pumped her fist in the air. "The Dynamic Duo will show off all our moves! We'll take on every jammer there!"

Her mom shook her head. "Hold up. That's not how it works in derby, kiddo. Five girls on the track at a time."

Kenzie's arm drifted down by her side.

"So?"

"So, when the league states that a group can try out, they mean a *team*. You'll need three more players."

*Three more players?*

Kenzie's knees suddenly felt like lumps of jelly. She sank facedown into the rug. Her dad leaned against the doorframe.

"Hey, that's not so bad," he said. "This is good news."

"But how am I supposed to find three more people?" Kenzie groaned into the floor. "The other kids at Free Skate are always making fun of us."

"Then roller derby isn't for them," her mom said.

"You could look outside of Free Skate," her dad suggested. "I'll bet a lot of kids at school and around the neighborhood don't know about derby. You could introduce them to it."

Verona walked into the living room and hovered over Kenzie. A piece of paper landed on Kenzie's back. The crayon bounced and landed next to her.

"Brainstorm!" Verona said.

"I agree," their dad said.

Kenzie rolled onto her side. She pinned the paper down over the hard part of the floor and wrote down the storm inside her head:

- Shelly and I can try out for derby as a team.
- Derby team = FIVE people.
- The Dynamic Duo = TWO people.
- We need THREE more players by Saturday.

Kenzie reread the list. Her thoughts didn't seem as scary written out in purple crayon.

*Three more players.*

Three was a pretty small number, if Kenzie thought about it. Verona learned how to count to three when she was still a baby. When Kenzie's dad gave her the good chores, he said they were easy as "one, two, three." How hard could it be to find three roller derby players?

Kenzie turned to her family and smiled.

"OK," she said. "The Dynamic Duo is forming a team!"

# CHAPTER THREE

THE NEXT AFTERNOON, KENZIE PERCHED ON HER favorite rock at the park downtown, waiting for Shelly.

Sundays were Shelly's only full day with her dad, which meant she usually didn't have time to meet. But Kenzie texted their secret emergency code—*M&M SOS!*—around lunch. Kenzie knew she was supposed to let Shelly hang out with her dad, but forming a derby team in six days was hard enough. They couldn't afford to lose any more time.

As she waited for Shelly to show, Kenzie watched a game of tag on the field. Every time a new person was tagged, the group of kids scattered in all directions. Some of them were really fast, Kenzie noticed. But they all looked too young to join derby.

She glanced at the playground. A couple of older boys

sat on the swings watching videos on their phones. Some smaller kids were shifting around huge piles of woodchips. One girl ran in circles spinning a roundabout as her friend crouched inside.

"I think I'm going to be sick!" the friend cried out.

Kenzie shook her head. That kid did not have the stomach for roller derby.

"Kenzilla!"

Shelly flew down the sidewalk and scrambled up to join Kenzie on the rock. They bumped fists twice and spit in opposite directions.

"What's the SOS?" Shelly asked.

Kenzie fished the brainstorm list out of her pocket and handed it over. Shelly read through the bullet points in Kenzie's purple scrawl.

"Three more players . . ." she murmured. She looked up at Kenzie. "We're forming a whole team? That's awesome!"

Kenzie smiled. She pictured skating next to Shelly around the track, leading a pack of rough-and-tough derby girls behind them. Their team would twirl and jump and spin in really fast circles and—

A worrying thought popped into her head.

"Hey, Shelly," Kenzie said.

"Yeah?"

"Tricks are really hard in derby."

Shelly nodded. Kenzie turned to her.

"*Skating* is really hard in derby."

"I guess," Shelly said. "What's your point?"

Kenzie knitted her hands together. "What if we can't find anyone who can skate backward or flip around? What if we have to do all the work for a whole team?"

Shelly swiped at the air.

"We'll find lots of girls just like us," she said. "Our team will be full of derby pros!"

"Maybe," Kenzie said, frowning a little. She wasn't sure if there were lots of girls like them.

"Do you have a pencil?" Shelly asked. "We can come up with some team names. That's how we'll advertise!"

Kenzie took a pencil from her pocket and handed it to Shelly. Shelly made a squiggly line under the purple crayon.

"The Scream Queens," Shelly said aloud as she wrote. She grinned at Kenzie. "And we can be known for screaming every time the whistle blows!"

"But that's only for our Banshee move," Kenzie reminded her. "How about the M&Ms?"

Since Kenzie's full name was Mackenzie and Shelly's name was Michelle, "M&M" was Kenzie and Shelly's special friend nickname.

"Hmmmm . . ." Shelly chewed on the eraser. "We might not get a team full of M names, though. Plus, in derby you're Kenzilla, not Mackenzie. And I'm Bomb Shell, not Michelle."

Kenzie stared at the ground. What Shelly said made sense. She liked being Kenzilla way better than she liked being Mackenzie. Still, something seemed wrong. Her heart stung, the way her finger stung when a splinter was hiding right under the skin. Shelly used to like being the M&Ms. What was different now?

"How about the Dynamic Duo?" Kenzie asked.

Shelly laughed. "Duo means 'two,'" she said. "You wrote it right here. Hey, maybe we could do something like that, but for five people. Like the Fierce Five, or the Ferocious Five."

"Ferocious?" a voice asked.

Kenzie and Shelly looked up just as Bree, Kenzie's neighbor, skidded to a stop in front of their rock. She kicked up her skateboard and caught it at her side.

"Can we help you?" Kenzie asked. She twisted to block the paper in Shelly's hands.

"Who's ferocious?" Bree asked.

"No one," Kenzie said right as Shelly yelled, "We are!"

"Ha!" Bree laughed. Her teeth glinted. "I've known Kenzie for a long time," she said. "But I never knew she was *ferocious*." Kenzie's pale cheeks turned bright red. She wished she had deep brown skin like Bree's so people wouldn't know every time she was embarrassed.

"Have you seen her on the derby track?" Shelly asked. "She's ferocious there. Hey! You should come to Free Skate nights sometime."

Bree spread her arms wide. "It's free

skating here. Why would I go skate in circles when I can board wherever I want?" She winked at Kenzie, then threw her skateboard in front of her and rolled down the sidewalk.

Kenzie's face burned an even brighter shade of red. She scowled at Shelly.

"Why did you have to tell her about Free Skate?"

"Why not?" Shelly asked. She watched as Bree disappeared around the corner. "She's really good. I'll bet she's good at skating too."

"I doubt it," Kenzie mumbled. "Skateboarding and roller skating are completely different."

She snatched the paper back from Shelly and hopped off the rock.

"Hey!" Shelly called. She followed Kenzie toward the playground. "Wait up!"

Kenzie dipped under the monkey bars and climbed up to the highest slide. Shelly paused at the bottom rung of the ladder. She shielded the sun from her eyes and shouted toward Kenzie.

"Why don't you like her?" Shelly asked.

Kenzie could feel her face turning red again. She thought about the way Bree winked right before she jumped on her skateboard. Why did Bree always make Kenzie so nervous? The feeling sloshed and bubbled in her stomach.

"I don't *not* like her. I don't like her *or* not like her. And that's not the point! Bree doesn't skate, and she thinks it's stupid. OK?"

She drew her legs in close to her chest.

Shelly climbed up the ladder and sat next to Kenzie.

"OK," Shelly said softly. They sat still together, listening to the shouts and cheers from the game of tag on the field. Shelly

leaned her head against Kenzie's shoulder. "So what kind of players do you want for the team?"

Kenzie let go of her knees and turned toward Shelly. "Well . . . you and I are both kind of short," she said. "So maybe someone tall."

"Good thinking," Shelly said. Kenzie smiled. The weird, unhappy splinter was starting to come out.

"How about someone to be our jammer?" Kenzie added. "Then they can focus on skating really fast, and we can focus on our blocking moves."

"That means we'd have to find someone even better at skating than us," Shelly said.

Both girls had to think about that one.

"Hey! You're holding up the slide."

Two younger kids from the game of tag stood at the base of the ladder.

Kenzie pushed herself forward and *whooshed* down the metal slope. Even though it was February, the slide was hot under her legs. Kenzie slowed down at the end, but before she could hoist herself off, Shelly came flying after.

"Look out!" Shelly called. "Bombs away!"

Shelly ran into Kenzie, and both girls sailed right into the giant pile of woodchips. They sat with their legs splayed out, giggling as they pulled woodchips from each other's hair.

"Hey!"

Kenzie looked up. The same boy was yelling again.

"We got out of your way," Kenzie said. "Slide all you want."

The boy cocked his head. "I wasn't talking to you." He tapped his friend's shoulder. "Who's that kid at the hoops?"

Both Kenzie and Shelly swiveled toward the other end of the park. A giant group of people was forming around the basketball court.

"What's going on?" Kenzie asked.

Shelly pushed herself up and pulled Kenzie after. "Let's go find out," she said with a grin.

# CHAPTER FOUR

**KENZIE AND SHELLY RAN TOWARD THE SHOUTS AND** cheers.

They rushed past squirrels chattering on tree branches and old couples reading side by side on benches. By the time they reached the court, they could only see the backs

of other kids. Kenzie heard hip-hop music blaring from a phone.

"Is someone dancing?" Shelly asked.

"I don't think so," Kenzie said.

They leaned in and listened. Under the sounds of music and yelling, they heard something *tap-tap-tap* against the concrete.

"It's dribbling," Kenzie said.

"Show 'em, girl!" someone yelled.

"That's it," Shelly said. "I'm going in."

She and Kenzie poked their way through the crowd. A tall, broad-shouldered girl stood at the center of the court. The basketball in her hands was a blur. It zipped from side to side, weaving under one leg and over her knee, around her waist and up over her head. She tossed the ball in an arc and

caught it behind her back. She closed her eyes, bounced the ball hard on the ground, turned in a circle, and caught it in one hand.

The crowd cheered. Kenzie and Shelly gaped at each other.

"Doesn't she go to our school?" Shelly asked.

Kenzie nodded. "Yeah, she's in my computer class. Her name's Tomoko, I think."

"I thought she was really shy," Shelly said.

"Me too."

They watched as Tomoko threw the ball in a perfect shot through the hoop. It didn't even touch the backboard.

"Nothing but net!" someone said.

Tomoko dribbled the ball fast between her legs. She bent her knees and cocked her arm back.

"Shoot! Shoot!" the kids chanted.

The music was ramping up. Kenzie closed her eyes and let the beat pulse through her. She could still see Tomoko behind her eyelids. But this Tomoko was decked out in crisp white roller skates.

"Skate! Skate!" the audience called.

Tomoko glided around the track, tossing the basketball and catching it again. She held the ball close to her and spun on one skate, around and around.

"Shoot it!" Shelly yelled.

Kenzie opened her eyes. If only Tomoko *could* skate. Then she would be perfect for the derby team.

Tomoko stepped back little by little until she was standing on the far side of the court. As the music swelled, she lined up her shot and flung the ball high. Everyone watched it arc through the air, spinning as if in slow motion.

The net sang as the ball dipped through—*Swish!*

The crowd went bonkers. "Wooooo!"

Tomoko made a small bow and jogged over to her basketball. As she picked it up again, the clapping faded and the music stopped. Kenzie watched the rest of the crowd scatter. A pack of boys with their own basketball rushed onto the court.

"Come on," Kenzie said. She tugged on Shelly's sleeve. "I think it's over. Let's get back to brainstorming team names."

Shelly turned. "We don't need the team name," she said excitedly.

"But what about advertising?" Kenzie asked.

"Don't you see?" Shelly said. "We don't need to advertise! We can get another player right now!"

"Who, Tomoko?" Kenzie pointed at the court. "But she doesn't skate!"

"Not *yet*," Shelly's eyes gleamed. "Maybe she'll want to!

"Didn't you see her out there?" she asked. "Tomoko's already great at getting crowds excited. All you have to do is put her in skates and *wa-bam!*—instant derby star! Can't you picture it?"

Kenzie paused. She thought of Tomoko in skates again, flying along the derby track. She smiled.

"I can picture it," Kenzie said.

She and Shelly turned back to the court. The group of boys had formed a circle.

"OK, teams," one boy said. He separated the others into two groups.

Tomoko emerged from the sideline. Her basketball was tucked under one arm.

"Which side am I on?" she asked.

The boy looked her over. "We already have enough players," he said gruffly. "It's even on both teams."

"But you're not on a team yet," Tomoko pointed out.

The boy rolled his eyes. He was tall, even taller than Tomoko. He was probably in sixth grade, Kenzie guessed. He exchanged a look with one of his friends. Tomoko's face was so hopeful. Kenzie wanted to hide. She hated seeing other people embarrassed almost as much as she hated being embarrassed.

"Look," the boy said to Tomoko, "you shoot good baskets. But when you play a basketball *game*, you need people who can *run*. And you're not really a runner. Sorry."

Tomoko's shoulders slumped.

"All right," the boy said, turning away from her, "which one of you cheeseballs is going to be ref so I can play?"

Shelly gritted her teeth and balled up a fist. "I'll show him."

"Wait," Kenzie said, grabbing Shelly's shoulder. "He's in middle school."

Kenzie watched as Tomoko shuffled down the sidewalk. "Let's help Tomoko instead."

Shelly didn't listen at first. She sent angry dragon breaths through her nostrils. She glared at the back of the boy's head, then slowly turned toward Tomoko.

"You're right," she said, softening. "Come on!"

Shelly bounded around the court. Kenzie followed her.

"Tomoko!" Shelly called. "Hey, Tomoko!"

Tomoko stopped walking, but she didn't turn around.

Shelly jumped in front of Tomoko. "That was awesome!"

"Oh. Thanks." Tomoko kept her chin nestled to her chest. She was back to being the shy girl Kenzie knew from class.

"Where did you learn how to do that?" Shelly asked.

Tomoko shrugged. "My uncle has a basketball hoop. He lets me practice in his driveway."

"You must really love basketball," Kenzie said as she joined them.

"Yeah . . . but basketball doesn't really love me," Tomoko muttered. She glanced over at the court.

"Forget those guys," Kenzie said. "They're jerks."

"They're totally jealous of you," Shelly added.

Tomoko sighed. "They never let me play on a team."

"Funny you should say that . . ." Shelly tried to throw an arm around Tomoko's shoulder, but Tomoko was so tall that it ended up on her back instead.

"As it so happens," Shelly said, "we have another team you might be interested in. Come with us."

Shelly ushered Tomoko out of the park, over toward South Congress Avenue, the main street bustling with shops. Kenzie followed behind. Sometimes, when Shelly got really excited, she exploded with energy. Kenzie could see Shelly's heels bouncing with each step. Hopefully she wouldn't scare Tomoko away from derby.

The three girls stopped at Kenzie and Shelly's favorite ice pop stand. The ice pop flavors were always weird combinations that no one else could think of.

"Give me three Sour Birthdays, please," Shelly said to

the man behind the counter. She turned to Tomoko. "You'll like it, I promise."

The man took out three speckled ice pops. Sour Birthday was Kenzie's favorite flavor. It was a mix of birthday cake, sea salt, and vinegar. She licked her lips as Shelly handed her an ice pop.

"You're a total star on the basketball court," Shelly said when they found a table. "But you need a better place to shine."

"What's the team?" Tomoko asked suspiciously. "Is it a basketball team?"

"Sort of," Shelly said. She took a large bite of the Sour Birthday. "But without the basketball."

Kenzie smacked her forehead. Tricking Tomoko into derby wasn't going to work.

"We're trying to form a roller derby team," she said. "You have to be on skates, and it's not that much like basketball."

"You *do* get to show off lots of tricks, though. Derby crowds love that kind of stuff," Shelly said.

Tomoko licked a corner of her ice pop. She wrinkled her nose. Kenzie crossed her fingers under the table.

"Skates, huh?" Tomoko said after a moment.

"Skates," Shelly echoed. "Which means no dumb boys talking about running. Heck, on skates you'd have them eating your dust."

Tomoko's eyes lit up.

"I like the sound of that," she said. "I'm in."

# CHAPTER FIVE

ON MONDAY MORNING, KENZIE WAITED OUTSIDE OF her classroom. Shelly bounced around the corner and collided into Kenzie's hip.

"Incoming!" Shelly cried.

Kenzie laughed and held out her hand. They bumped fists and pretended to spit (since actual spitting wasn't allowed in the hallway), then ducked into their M&M morning hideout, the bathroom.

"Do you think I could pull off a fauxhawk at derby practice?" Shelly asked, looking in the mirror.

"If most of your hair was gone, sure," Kenzie said. She pulled her own hair tight at the sides and pushed the middle up until she looked like a horse with a mane. "Like this," she said.

Shelly laughed and pushed her own hair up. "Hey! That could be our team name. The Fauxhawks."

"I'm not sure Tomoko would go for that," Kenzie said.

A muffled sound came from one of the stalls. Shelly let go of her hair.

"Tomoko?"

The door squeaked open. Tomoko peered out nervously.

"Hey!" Shelly said. "We were just talking about you! Come hang out with us at lunch today."

Shelly tapped Tomoko's elbow with her knuckle, but Kenzie noticed Tomoko dip away. Tomoko seemed a lot quieter now that they were back at school. They would need to work on pulling out her derby attitude.

At lunch, Kenzie and Shelly showed Tomoko how to press your finger over the water spout and squirt people. At recess, they showed her their invisible hopscotch obstacle-course game. After school as they walked downtown, Shelly demonstrated how to play hot lava on the sidewalk.

"You have to use stuff like bike racks and light poles. Watch this!" Shelly cried. She swung around and hopped onto a sewer grate.

"Uh-huh," Tomoko said.

Kenzie watched Tomoko carefully. She hid under her backpack like a turtle. Where was all the star power from the basketball court? Kenzie was starting to worry that Tomoko had changed her mind about joining the team.

"This is my block," Tomoko said. She hitched her thumb toward a side street.

"Bye!" Shelly called. She flapped her arm back and forth. "Don't step on the lava!"

Tomoko hardly waved back as she turned around the corner.

Kenzie looked at Shelly.

"We have to do something," Kenzie said. "Tomoko seems so shy around us."

"Are you thinking what I'm thinking?" Shelly asked.

The girls closed their eyes. Sometimes, when Kenzie and Shelly really focused, they could leave their regular brains behind and jump into one brain, the M&M brain.

"We were shy when we were little—" Shelly began.

"Because we didn't have each other," Kenzie added.

"Right," Shelly said. She paused. "Tomoko needs a friend. Like, a good friend."

Kenzie nodded. It wasn't easy having three people in a Dynamic Duo. But maybe once another person joined the team, she could be Tomoko's friend. She could even be her best friend! Then there would be *two* Dynamic Duos.

"It's a plan," Kenzie said. She opened her eyes. Shelly was already looking back at her.

*Operation Double Dynamic Duo.*

The girls bumped fists and spit into the lava.

The next day, Kenzie walked to school alongside Verona. Kenzie scrunched her mouth in concentration. She was hard at work coming up with plans to help Tomoko with her own Dynamic Duo.

Verona skipped ahead. "Greetings and salutations!" she sang out.

She waved at everyone they passed on South Congress between their apartment and school. She waved at the manager of the fancy hotel. She waved at the hostess of the café that had "the best bagels in Austin," according to their dad. She waved at the man who owned the flower shop, and the couple who ran a shop that only sold cowboy shirts and miniature cat paintings.

"Greetings and salutations!"

"Greetings and salutations!"

"Greetings and salutations!"

"Would you cut it out already?" Kenzie said. Her brain was twisted in knots from imagining how to find their next player for the team. She kicked a rock that bounced back on her toe.

Verona gripped her backpack straps and stuck her nose in the air.

"Everyone is my friend," she said. "And you always say hello to your friends."

"Just say hello then," Kenzie said. "No one says 'Greetings and salutations.'"

Verona looked at Kenzie very seriously. "They do in the book Ms. Sigler is reading to us," she said.

Kenzie rolled her eyes and followed Verona the rest of the way down the block. The girls hopped up the school steps and made their way to the kindergarten wing. Verona hugged Kenzie's waist.

"Greetings and salutations," she said. "That means good-bye too." She turned and ran to a group of kids inside her classroom. Kenzie sighed. Even though Verona could be annoying, she was really good at making friends. Kenzie was so used to being an M&M that she had almost forgotten how to make new friends. She needed some of Verona's skills if she was going to help Tomoko form her own duo. Or maybe even trio, since they needed two more players.

At lunch, Kenzie, Shelly, and Tomoko sat together. The cafeteria was filled with smells of garlic bread and spaghetti sauce. Tomoko poked at the pile of spaghetti on her tray. Shelly shoved half a meatball sub into her mouth. Kenzie munched on her own sub and peered around the lunchroom. She snuck looks up and down the lunch line and over the tables. There *had* to be someone else to add to the team.

"Have you ever roller-skated before?" Shelly asked Tomoko. She finished the last of her sandwich and licked her thumbs.

Tomoko looked up from her spaghetti.

"I think so," she said. "But it was a long time ago. Is that OK?"

"Of course!" Shelly said. "We just need to find a couple people who have skated a lot. To make things even. Like a certain person at the park . . ."

Shelly looked at Kenzie and wiggled her eyebrows.

"What person at the park?" Tomoko asked.

"Oh, just this girl Kenzie doesn't like," Shelly said.

"That's not true," Kenzie said. "I like Bree. I just don't like her as a friend."

As soon as the words were out of her mouth, Kenzie froze. Her heart raced behind her sandwich. Did she just say what she thought she said? She looked across the table. Shelly was busy inhaling her dessert. But Tomoko was looking right back at Kenzie.

"What does that mean?" Tomoko asked.

"Nothing," Kenzie said quickly. She wasn't going to explain the jitters she felt every time she looked at Bree. Tomoko didn't even know Bree.

"It doesn't mean anything." Kenzie forced herself to take another bite. "We need to get looking for more people," she said between chews. "I was thinking we could try—"

The lights flicked off and then on again. The chatter in the room died down.

"Draw if you be men!"

Two girls stood up in the middle of the cafeteria, each

holding a wooden ruler toward the other. They tapped their rulers back and forth, as if they were sword fighting.

"What's going on?" Kenzie whispered.

"I think it's the drama club," Tomoko said. She pointed to the doors, where the drama teacher stood with her arms folded, smiling.

Kenzie nodded. She watched the girls wave the rulers around.

One of the girls had long, shiny brown hair. She held her ruler lightly. The other girl was small, with frizzy blond hair that hovered over her like a tumbleweed. The smaller girl jumped and dove across the tables.

"Hi-yah!" she yelled with each move.

A boy suddenly stepped between the outstretched rulers. He opened his arms wide.

"Part fools! Put up your swords. You know not what you do."

The girl with long hair let her ruler fall at her side, but the shorter girl lunged across the boy, her ruler outstretched.

"En garde!" she yelled.

"Jules, that's not the line," the boy said.

"How dare you insult the Montagues?" the small girl cried. "Fight or be a coward!" She prodded her opponent with the end of her ruler.

The other girl turned to the drama teacher. "Miss Moss, she's changing it again!"

"Cut," Miss Moss called hurriedly. She clapped her hands together like she wanted everyone to join in, but only a few kids applauded. "Look out for our upcoming production of Shakespeare's *Romeo and Juliet*," she announced to the room. Her voice dropped to a low growl as she turned to Jules. "My office. Now."

The cafeteria had gone completely quiet. Kenzie watched wide-eyed as Jules strode to the doors. She didn't even seem embarrassed.

"This Shakespeare dude's got it all wrong," Jules said. "What's the point of putting a sword fight in the play and calling it off after two seconds?"

No one got to hear the drama teacher's answer. She whisked Jules out into the hall. The doors flapped back and forth behind them. After a moment, the room exploded in voices. Pairs of kids picked up their stale chunks of garlic bread and thwacked them together.

"Draw if you be men!"

"Can you imagine if she had a real sword?"

"Miss Moss would have to call an ambulance!"

"Whoa," Shelly said, turning back to the table. "That kid was nuts."

"Are you kidding?" Kenzie grinned and set down her sandwich. "That kid is going to be our next team member!"

# CHAPTER SIX

**THE WAREHOUSE SPEAKER CRACKLED ON IN KENZIE'S** head.

"Attention derby devotees, skating supporters, athlete aficionados," the announcer crooned. "Introducing our newest player to the track. Part roller girl. Part stage diva. The one. The only. The bejeweled Jules!"

Jules, her hair wilder than ever, wheeled across the derby rink. She was in full Shakespearean costume, with emerald roller skates that matched her tights. Her sword clanged and shone as she slashed it through the air. The derby crowd threw roses at her feet.

"Bravo!" the crowd yelled.

Kenzie pushed her food away and stood up from the table.

"I'm going to talk to Jules," she said to Shelly and Tomoko. "Before she gets detention, at least."

"Want this?" Shelly held up her spoon. "You might need it to win her over."

Tomoko laughed. Kenzie rolled her eyes and waved the spoon away. She threaded through the tables and turned into the hall, her shoes squeaking against the linoleum.

Maybe Jules *was* a little out there. Maybe she didn't follow the script exactly. Maybe she was too rowdy for being in plays.

But that's what made her great for derby.

Kenzie's squeaky steps echoed as she crept farther down the hall toward the auditorium. Lunch still wasn't out yet, and if she got caught sneaking around, she might land herself in trouble right alongside Jules. The door to Miss Moss's office was slightly open. An angry-sounding voice drifted out.

"I have to get special permission for us to perform scenes during the school day," Miss Moss said. "The principal is putting a lot of trust in us. If you touch another student with *anything*, I'll have to report that as actual fighting, and next time you'll go straight to his office. Do you understand?"

Kenzie leaned toward the doorway.

"Yes," Jules said. She paused. "But I was only trying to make the play more realistic. I mean, if the Montagues and

Capulets are already getting mad at each other, I don't think they would stop fighting just because some guy called them 'fools.'"

A long sigh came from the office.

"Just give me the ruler and we'll talk about this after school."

"Fine," Jules muttered. The ruler clacked onto the desk. Kenzie heard a chair scrape against the floor. Her heart jumped in her chest. What if the teacher saw her waiting outside? She scrambled toward the main hallway, searching for a broom closet to run into or trash can to hide behind.

"What are you doing?"

Kenzie turned. Jules stood in the hall, her hand on the doorknob.

"Who's out there?" Miss Moss asked.

Jules looked at Kenzie for a moment. "No one," she said. "Just my imaginary friend."

The drama teacher sighed again. Jules closed the door the rest of the way.

Kenzie signaled Jules to stay quiet as they crept around the corner. They found a door that opened onto the playground, where everyone would come streaming as soon as lunch let out. The girls crouched under a big tree. The branches did a pretty good job of hiding them, at least for the next few minutes.

"What were you doing back there?" Jules asked. She raised an eyebrow. "Spying on me?"

"Sort of," Kenzie admitted. "I really liked your sword fight."

Jules picked up a twig and twirled it in her hand. "Yeah? I practiced way more moves at home, but Miss Moss never lets me use them in scenes."

"I think the sword fighting is more fun to watch than the talking, anyway," Kenzie said. "Do you know how to sword fight for real?"

"I wish," Jules said. She tossed the twig to the side. "It's fun to pretend, though. That's why I joined drama club in the first place, when I saw the sword fighting."

"Do you like acting?" Kenzie asked.

Jules shrugged. "It's OK," she said. "I had wanted to go out for football, but they don't let girls on the team."

Kenzie grinned and squeezed her hands together. Sword fighting? *Football?* She could hardly keep from flapping her arms around the way Shelly did when she was really excited. Jules was perfect for derby.

Hopefully she would also be perfect for Tomoko.

The bell rang inside the building. Five seconds later, the first wave of fifth graders rushed onto the playground. Now Kenzie and Jules were free to go where they wanted. But Kenzie had to get Jules to say yes before she brought her back to the group.

Kenzie stood up and dusted off her pants, then offered a hand to Jules. "Have you ever thought about knocking people around on wheels?"

"Like in go-carts?"

"Nope. On skates. You would make a great derby player."

Jules still looked confused. "I thought derby was in go-carts," she said. "Or on horses or something."

"I'm talking about roller derby," Kenzie said. "You'd be on skates, and it's a lot more like football than like go-carts."

She took off toward the swings. "Come on, I'll show you one of our moves."

Kenzie approached the swing at the far end of the playground. She gripped the chains, then stepped onto the seat. Jules hoisted herself onto the swing next to Kenzie's.

"Why are we standing on the swings?"

"You'll see. Move your weight from one foot to the other," Kenzie said. "Then stick your hips out side to side. See if you can move the swing without stepping down and pushing."

EEEAK

CREEEAK

CREEEEEAK...

Jules shook the chains hard for a minute, but all that did was make her wiggle in place. She jabbed her shoulders out. She flapped her elbows like a chicken.

"Use your legs," Kenzie instructed. "Try to be like one of those clocks that swings back and forth."

Jules paused. She took a breath, then leaned to the left. She jerked and leaned to the right. She leaned to the left again. The swing was starting to move.

"Good job!" Kenzie said. "Now stick your hips out. Try to touch my swing."

*Creeeeaaaak. Creeeeaaaak.*

The chains moaned as Jules shifted her swing closer and closer. Jules huffed and pulled herself back and forth, back and forth, until finally—*boop!* Her hip tapped Kenzie's.

"Yes!" Kenzie said.

Jules let her swing hang down again. "What was that for?"

"That was a hip check," Kenzie explained. "In derby, a bunch of kids put on skates and go around a track. The whole time they're trying to knock each other down, but they can't use their hands. Only their hips. They're called hip checks, and they're really hard to practice since you only use your leg muscles. Your arms are mostly there for balance."

"Hip checks?" Jules blinked. Her eyes were wide and bright.

Kenzie laughed. "I knew you'd like it. My best friend and I are forming a team, and we start on Saturday. You should join!"

She paused a moment. "Also, you would love Tomoko. She plays basketball, and she's so much better than the teams that play at the park. She's really tough, like you, and she's just starting on skates."

"Tomoko's your best friend?" Jules asked.

"What? No. That's Shelly. She's . . ." Kenzie thought about all the amazing things she could say about Shelly. But then she remembered the Dynamic Duo plan. She had to find Tomoko a best friend so she would feel better about the team. Jules didn't need to know so much about Shelly.

"She's cool too, I guess," Kenzie said. "So what do you think? You want to come play derby with us?"

Jules rested her chin in her hand. "Hmmm," she murmured. "We're supposed to practice more scenes from *Romeo and Juliet* this weekend."

Kenzie's shoulders sagged. "Oh. I get it."

"Hold on," Jules said. "I haven't decided yet. The truth is, I think Miss Moss wants to replace me anyway. She says it would be better if my character didn't hold any weapons. But I've never even hurt anyone! And what's the fun of Shakespeare without a sword?"

She tapped her chin.

Kenzie held her breath.

"Oh, what the heck," Jules said. "Derby sounds awesome!"

"Yes!" Kenzie hopped out of her swing. "Come on, let's go find the others!"

By now the whole fifth grade was swarming over the playground. Two girls grabbed Kenzie's and Jules's swings before they even let go of the chains. Kenzie was too excited to care. Now that Jules was in the group, Kenzie and Shelly were only one player away from a whole team. And even better, Tomoko would have her own best friend to help her come out of her turtle shell. Everything was working out perfectly.

Kenzie and Jules waded through the crowds. Kenzie heard basketballs bouncing over the court. Maybe Tomoko was practicing basketball. She made her way under the hoops, but neither Tomoko nor Shelly was there. Kenzie heard a laugh that sounded a lot like Shelly's. She looked around.

Under a tree near the building, exactly where Kenzie and Jules had been sitting before the bell rang, Shelly and

Tomoko were huddled close together. Shelly tapped her knuckles to Tomoko's, then spit over her shoulder.

Kenzie's throat went dry. The invisible splinter in her heart throbbed with pain. She hunched over. She and Shelly were supposed to be finding Tomoko a *new* best friend. Not showing her all of their secret M&M moves. What was going on?

"What is it?" Jules asked. "Did you lose something?"

Kenzie rubbed the sting out of her eyes. She glanced at her best friend again.

"I hope not," she said.

# CHAPTER SEVEN

**KENZIE STARED AT HER CEILING THE NEXT MORNING** for a very long time. Staring at the ceiling was a lot like staring at clouds, because she always saw different shapes pop out from the textured plaster. Today, Kenzie saw two hands high-five each other. She thought about Shelly and Tomoko bumping fists and spitting over their shoulders.

How could Shelly have gotten the Double Dynamic Duo plan so wrong? They had jumped into the M&M brain. They came up with the idea together! Usually Shelly and Kenzie were on the same page about everything. But the derby team was throwing them off. What if the closer they got to a team, the further away they got from their own Dynamic Duo?

Kenzie shuddered.

"I see you've decided on breakfast to go."

Kenzie's dad popped his head in the doorway. He held a banana in one hand and a granola bar in the other.

Kenzie closed her eyes and pulled the covers up to her nose. "I decided on breakfast in bed."

She waited for her dad to leave.

"It's only Wednesday," he said. "You still have plenty of time to find two more people."

"One more person," Kenzie said. "I found someone yesterday."

*Who was supposed to be Tomoko's best friend*, she added in her head.

"Even better," her dad said cheerfully. "Let's celebrate in the kitchen! Over breakfast."

Kenzie grumbled as her dad disappeared back into the hall. She scooched out of bed and threw on some jeans and one of her mom's old derby T-shirts. Her feet dragged as she walked into the kitchen, where Verona was building a tower from banana slices and their mom hovered over the blender. Kenzie sat next to her dad and rested her cheek on the table. He nudged the granola bar and banana toward her.

"Why the long face?" Kenzie's mom asked.

Kenzie shrugged and unpeeled her banana.

"Don't look at me," her dad said. "Apparently finding derby players is bad news now."

Kenzie's mom looked quizzically at Kenzie, but Kenzie pretended to be busy eating her banana. She wasn't ready to explain everything going on.

She slipped on her backpack, then hugged her dad good-bye at the door. He always left first since he had to drive to a tall office building across the river. Kenzie liked not having to drive anywhere. The walk to school always gave her time to think, and this morning, she had a lot of thinking to do.

"I'll walk with you two," her mom said. "At least until the Yarn Shop. I'm opening today."

As her mom walked and her sister skipped and waved to every person ever, Kenzie trudged behind them. Her eyes stayed on the ground. She imagined one of her sneakers as Shelly and the other sneaker as Tomoko. She kept her feet very far apart.

"Are the new girls nice?" her mom asked over her shoulder.

"Uh-huh," Kenzie said.

"Does Shelly get along with them too?"

Kenzie took an extra-wide step. "Maybe a little too well," she muttered.

"I see."

Kenzie's mom didn't ask any more questions.

The girls hugged their mom at the shop doors. As Kenzie pulled away, her mom tugged on Kenzie's sleeve.

"Hey," she said. "I could really use some company at derby practice tonight. How about you take a break from team planning and come with me?"

Kenzie's eyes lit up. "Can I practice too?"

"Not on the track," her mom said. "But you can skate on the sidelines."

"Deal," Kenzie said. She waved to her mom and caught up with Verona.

"Salutations!" Verona called toward the shop.

Kenzie kept her chin high the rest of the walk to school. Going to a real derby practice was exactly what she needed. The only reason she and Shelly were making a team anyway was so they could play derby together. Not to break up the Dynamic Duo. Shelly would remember that as soon as they slid their skates back on and flew into formation.

"Kenzilla!" Shelly said as Kenzie rounded the corner. Tomoko was standing awfully close to Shelly's shoulder.

"Hey, Bomb Shell," Kenzie said. She held out her hand for a fist bump.

"And?" Shelly asked. She looked at Tomoko expectantly, but Tomoko blushed.

"I don't know yet," she said. "Just Tomoko is fine."

"Just Tomoko? *Just* Tomoko?! You need a derby name," Shelly said. "Something strong, and maybe a little scary."

"Then I'll be the WRECKING BALL!"

Jules elbowed between Tomoko and Shelly and crashed into the group. Tomoko jumped back. Kenzie laughed.

"Shelly and I used our real names to make derby names," Kenzie said, "but it's a good start. Shelly, Tomoko, this is Jules, our newest member."

Tomoko raised her eyebrows. "So that's where you were after lunch."

Kenzie nodded. She didn't say anything about what she had seen on the playground.

"Are you a skater?" Shelly asked eagerly.

Jules shook her head. "No," she said. "But I already learned hip checks."

"And she's really good," Kenzie added. "Already. She's got the hip swing down."

Shelly didn't look so sure, but she pressed her mouth into a tight smile.

"OK," she said.

"That means both you and Tomoko are beginners. But if we get in a practice or two before Saturday, we should be in good shape. Let's try some moves at the courts after school."

"I can't today," Kenzie said. "My mom has derby practice."

"Sweet," Shelly said. "We can all go to the warehouse!"

Kenzie swallowed. She glanced at Tomoko. "Well, actually, I don't think I can bring other people."

Shelly stared at Kenzie like her head was on sideways. Even her freckles looked confused. "What are you talking about?" she asked.

Kenzie thought about what her mom had said that morning. She needed a break from all this team stuff, the handshake stuff, and maybe . . . *maybe* that also meant she needed a break from Shelly.

"Sorry," Kenzie said. She slipped away from the group just as the first bell rang, but she could still feel Shelly's eyes digging into her.

"Quick recover! Quick recover! Get your legs back under you!" Mambo Rambo shouted.

The Glitter Gals and Hazel Nuts were doing drills together. All around the track, derby players dropped to the ground and popped back up again. Off the track,

Kenzie was practicing with them. Falling fast was easy, but getting up fast was another story.

"And one—drop! Two—up! Get your balance!"

After what seemed like a million times of falling and then scrambling to stand, Mambo clapped her hands.

"Water break!" she called. "Five minutes."

Kenzie's mom sat down on the bench next to Kenzie.

"How are you holding up?" she asked.

"OK, I guess," Kenzie said. She wiped the sweat from her eyes. "I didn't know Mambo was the coach for the Glitter Gals."

Her mom grinned. "She's not," she said. "She's practicing for Saturday."

Kenzie waited for her mom to explain what that meant. Then she remembered what was happening on Saturday.

"Wait. She's the junior league coach?"

"One of them," her mom said. She grabbed a towel and patted it around her neck, then passed the towel to Kenzie. "So," she said, "tell me what's going on with Shelly."

Kenzie sighed. "Shelly showed our handshake to one of the new girls."

"The M&M handshake?" her mom asked.

"Yep," Kenzie said. "Which is our special handshake. Not a team handshake!"

"Your team has a handshake already?" Kenzie looked up as Mambo stepped off the track. "That was some nice hustling over there during drills. You ready for Saturday?"

"I'm glad you're coaching," Kenzie said. She bit her lip. "But Shelly and I aren't ready . . . not yet, anyway. We still need one more person."

"That's not what I mean," Mambo said. "I'm sure you and Shelly will fill your team. Being ready in derby isn't about numbers, or even about training. It's about rolling with the punches."

"What kind of punches?" Kenzie asked.

Mambo sat on the bleachers.

"Oh, anything," she said. "Trading positions. Throwing out plays. A teammate getting benched. You have to be ready for change."

Kenzie's legs dangled over the bleacher. Her skates rolled back and forth beneath her. She wondered what it would be like to skate with a whole group of people instead of just Shelly at her side.

"What if I'm not ready for change?" she asked carefully.

Mambo smiled. She gave Kenzie's shoulder a soft jab.

"Change happens no matter what, Kenzilla—you can't control that. The thing to focus on is how you pivot and skate forward. All right, y'all! Another round! Let's go!"

She stood and blew her whistle, then looked back at Kenzie.

"You up for another challenge?"

# CHAPTER EIGHT

KENZIE AND HER MOM DRAGGED THEMSELVES OUT OF the warehouse an hour later. Their cheeks were flushed. Their hair clung to their foreheads.

It had been a good practice.

"Still upset about the handshake?" Kenzie's mom asked as they walked home.

"I guess, yeah," Kenzie answered. "It's just . . . the M&M stuff is supposed to be secret. Shelly telling everyone makes it seem like she doesn't care at all."

Her mom thought for a moment.

"Maybe Shelly wanted the others to feel included," she said. "And that's why she shared the handshake."

"But that wasn't the plan," Kenzie said. "We were supposed to find a new friend for Tomoko, so she could have her own Dynamic Duo."

Kenzie's mom raised an eyebrow. "And what were you going to do once a fifth person joined the team?"

Kenzie searched her head for an answer. Her mom slid an arm around her.

"All I'm saying is, try not to break five people into two and two. Or two and three. Let five people be five people. Have fun with the whole group."

Kenzie sighed. Her mom just didn't understand.

As they walked together, they passed by the park. Shelly was perched on the M&M meeting rock.

Kenzie stopped.

"Would it be OK if—"

Her mom held out an arm. "Give me the skates. Go see your friend. Everything's going to work itself out."

Kenzie shifted her pair of skates from her shoulder to her mom's. She draped her helmet strap over her mom's wrist and planted a kiss on her palm.

"Thanks!"

Her mom smiled. "You're welcome. And hey, don't forget what Mambo said about change."

"Right," Kenzie said. She ran across the field, toward the

playground. Shelly sat cross-legged at the top of their rock. She didn't have a book with her, and her phone wasn't out on her lap.

"What are you doing up there?" Kenzie asked. "Bird-watching?"

Shelly smiled, but not in her usual peppy way.

"People-watching," she said. "For another member."

Kenzie climbed to the top of the rock next to Shelly. It seemed quieter up here, away from screaming little kids and barking dogs. Kenzie felt quieter too.

"I should have taken you to practice," Kenzie said. She cradled her knees in front of her. "I just didn't want to bring everyone."

Kenzie tapped into the M&M brain, imagining all the things Shelly might say back.

*That's OK.*

*Four people is a lot.*

*It's always been our thing anyway.*

"I think next time we should all go," Shelly actually said.

Kenzie blinked. Why was Shelly acting so different? Didn't she miss the Dynamic Duo?

Before Kenzie could respond, she heard a low rumble vibrating from the sidewalk. She would know that rumbling anywhere.

Bree.

*Great*, Kenzie thought. It was hard enough dealing with best friend troubles. She didn't need another round of stomach jitters.

Bree shot out from around the curve and came swerving down the sidewalk toward them. She was always out here, Kenzie realized. Always on her skateboard. Bree was more focused than any other kid Kenzie knew. That's what made her so cool.

Suddenly Kenzie felt Shelly's hand cup over hers.

"It's a sign," Shelly said.

"It is?" Kenzie asked. "Of what?"

Shelly turned to Kenzie and grinned. "Now that we're down to the last team member, we *need* someone who knows how to skate. Your neighbor—"

"Bree," Kenzie said.

"Bree could totally trade in her skateboard for skates! And she's passing us again, like she knew we would be here. Are you thinking what I'm thinking?"

Kenzie sighed. She didn't even

bother to close her eyes. The M&M brain wasn't working the way it used to. Every idea Shelly had was like the opposite of Kenzie's idea.

"I don't know about this . . ." Kenzie began. But Shelly jumped down and landed on the sidewalk just in front of Bree.

"Hey!" Shelly said.

Bree angled her skateboard toward the grass and hopped off to the side.

"You can't stand in front of moving wheels like that," she said. "You'll make me crash."

"Oh. Sorry!" Shelly picked up Bree's board and held it out to her. "You know . . . roller skates are like mini skateboards for your feet."

Bree put her hands on her hips. "Is this another invite to Free Skate?"

"No," Shelly said. "It's an invite to roller derby! Kenzie and I want you on our team!"

Kenzie shuffled from the rock until she stood just behind Shelly. Bree locked eyes with Kenzie over Shelly's shoulder.

"Is that so?" Bree asked. "You want me to downgrade to skates?"

"Skates aren't a downgrade," Kenzie said. She cleared her throat. "I mean, roller derby is an upgrade."

Bree grinned. "Skateboarders don't go around in circles like hamsters." She spun her finger around and around.

Kenzie rolled her eyes. "You do too," she said. "You're always going around the park. And you skate here because you like to skate in front of people. Roller derby players skate in front of huge crowds of screaming fans."

"In a bunch of elbow pads," Bree said.

"Because they're knocking into each other," Kenzie shot back. "Roller derby is way tougher than skateboarding."

Bree laughed, but it didn't seem like a mean laugh. The heat that normally sat in Kenzie's cheeks radiated through her arms and legs. She liked talking to Bree like this.

"Yeah, maybe," Bree said. "But those chicks slam into their own friends. I don't want to play derby with someone who doesn't like me from the start."

Kenzie stopped. Her smile fell.

"You think I don't like you?" Kenzie asked.

Now it was Bree's turn to go quiet. She looked at Kenzie, then looked away.

Shelly stepped forward.

"She does too like you," Shelly said. "She just doesn't like you as a friend."

Time slowed down after Shelly spoke. Her words landed with a heavy thud, right between Bree and Kenzie.

*She likes you. Not as a friend.*

"What?" Bree took a step back.

Kenzie's head went fuzzy. She couldn't think straight.

"She means—I meant—" Kenzie started to say. But she didn't get to finish. Bree hopped onto her skateboard. Kenzie watched as she disappeared around the corner.

"Bummer," Shelly said.

Kenzie turned. "Why did you have to say all that?"

"What?" Shelly said indignantly. "I was trying to explain that you guys didn't have to be *friends*, but you could be good *teammates*."

"Teammates?" Kenzie shook her head. "She thinks I have a crush on her!"

Shelly froze. She seemed almost dumbfounded.

"Why would she think that?"

Kenzie's mouth hung open. She couldn't find a single word to help her answer. Shelly was messing up everything that used to be normal. The M&Ms were different. Things with Bree were different. Mambo Rambo had said derby players needed to be ready for change . . . but that didn't mean Kenzie had to like what was changing.

Kenzie took a very deep breath. She tried to swallow all the bad thoughts in her head. Then, before she could stop herself, she exhaled.

"Because I— Bree— Because you're ruining everything, that's why!" Kenzie screamed. She turned and ran out of the park before Shelly could see her cry.

# CHAPTER NINE

MAMBO'S VOICE ECHOED IN KENZIE'S HEAD THE NEXT morning.

*One—drop!*

"Ugh," Kenzie groaned. She rolled out of bed and onto the floor. She felt like she'd hardly slept. She had tossed and turned all night, her brain replaying the scene at the park over and over.

*Two—up!*

Kenzie slid her backpack on at the front door. Why did she have to explode at Shelly like that? Why couldn't Kenzie just tell her about the feelings she got whenever Bree was around? Kenzie was used to sharing secrets with Shelly, not keeping them from her. But things with Tomoko and the team were getting so complicated. Mambo was right:

Kenzie had to skate forward. If she and Shelly were going to play derby, that meant they needed to work together.

Which also meant Kenzie needed to apologize.

"Hey." Kenzie stopped in front of her classroom. Shelly stood in their usual spot. Her brow was furrowed.

"Are you talking to me?" she asked. "Or to someone who hasn't ruined everything?"

"I'm sorry," Kenzie said. "After what happened with Bree, I was really embarrassed. But I shouldn't have said that to you."

Shelly pressed her lips together. "You were the one who said you didn't like Bree as a friend," she said. "I didn't think you had a crush on her. And it's really important to get another skater for the team."

Kenzie hung her head. All her feelings were wrapped tightly together like strings that had gotten tangled in a drawer. If Kenzie told Shelly the truth about Bree . . . then she might spill everything bothering her about Tomoko and the M&M handshake, and the team would fall apart before they even got started.

"I don't have a crush on anyone," Kenzie said, swallowing her secret inside her. She was beginning to understand a little bit better how her dad felt in his "before" stories.

Shelly squinted at Kenzie like she was reading something on her forehead. She still looked a little mad.

"We'll find another skater for the team. Today. I promise." Kenzie offered her hand to Shelly. Shelly paused for a moment, then bumped Kenzie's fist.

"OK," Shelly said. "Let's do this."

Kenzie grinned.

Tomoko and Jules came around the corner.

"The rest of Team Derby!" Shelly said. The girls all tapped hands.

"I don't think that'll stick," Tomoko said. "All the basketball teams I know have real names."

Kenzie glanced at Shelly. Since they were the ones who formed the team, they should be the ones to come up with a name. Not Tomoko.

"Let's wait until we get a full team first," Shelly said.

Kenzie nodded.

"Speaking of a full team," Jules said, "any ideas on where we're going to find our last member?"

The girls all waited for someone else to come up with a plan.

"Hey! Maybe we should brainstorm," Shelly said.

Jules grimaced. "I thought teachers came up with brain-storming as a torture device."

"No," Shelly said. "Kenzie's mom has us do it all the time, and it works! That's how we got the idea to form a derby team in the first place. Come on, let's go to the meeting spot."

Shelly turned for the bathroom. Kenzie paused a moment, then followed with the rest. Since when did the bathroom become the team meeting spot?

The door closed behind Kenzie. Shelly, Tomoko, and Jules

stood in a semicircle by the sink in the corner. A girl at the middle sink eyed them as she wrestled her hair into a bun.

"Come on," Shelly said, waving Kenzie over. "Only ten minutes until class starts."

Kenzie swung her backpack around and unzipped the main pocket. She reached deep in her pack, way past her notebooks, to the black hole where graded spelling tests and unfinished activity sheets liked to vanish. She fished out a crumpled ball of paper that turned out to be a parent permission slip she thought she lost three months ago. She smoothed it out and flipped it to the blank side. Jules handed over a pencil that was barely longer than Kenzie's pinkie finger. Kenzie looked at Jules.

"What?" Jules said. "I like my pencils extra sharp."

"OK," Shelly said. "List time. We need to find someone who's skated before. What are some ways we can get our last member?"

"Ooh! I've got one," Jules said. Everyone turned to her. "It starts like this: First, we prank-call the secretary and tell her to come see something going on at the playground. Then, while she's gone, we sneak past her desk and break into the principal's office. We take over that thing with the huge speakers. What's it called?"

"The intercom?" Kenzie asked.

"Yeah," Jules said, "the intercom. Then, when it's time

for morning announcements, we'll tell the whole school about roller derby! I'll bet we could get at least one skater to come to practice that way."

The others stared at Jules.

"That's your idea?" Tomoko said.

Jules nodded.

*Intercom takeover*, Kenzie wrote on the list.

"I don't even know where to start about how bad that plan is," Tomoko said.

"It's a great plan!" Jules huffed. "If you think it's so awful, you come up with something."

"What if we had a bake sale?" Shelly said. "And then we could use the money to pay someone."

"They should want to be on the team without being paid," Kenzie said. She wondered if Shelly was thinking of Bree specifically.

Even though Kenzie didn't think they needed to raise money, she still wrote *Bake sale* down. That was one of the rules of brainstorming: No idea was too out there to go on the list.

"We can't really do a bake sale in one day anyway," Tomoko said. "I don't think complicated ideas are going to work."

"The whole point of brainstorming is to get lots of ideas," Shelly said. "Then you can cross things off later."

"Yeah," Jules said. "You still haven't added anything."

Tomoko sighed. "OK," she said. "There's this thing in basketball right when the buzzer's about to go off and the quarter is over. Whoever has the ball, even if they're way on the other side of the court, has to throw it at their basket."

"And?" Shelly said.

"It's called a *Hail Mary*," Tomoko explained. "And most of the time the ball doesn't make it through the hoop. But once in a blue moon, the Hail Mary works and you get the shot. I think we need a lot of Hail Marys today."

*Hail Mary*, Kenzie wrote on the list.

"So we're throwing things at people?" Jules asked.

"No," Tomoko said. "We ask a bunch of kids about derby. Like, as many kids as possible. And we hope that one—a skater—says yes."

"I like it!" Shelly said. "Let's go with that idea first. Talk to as many people as you can in class, over lunch, and at recess."

Kenzie shrugged. It wasn't the worst idea in the world.

The girls threw their hands into the circle between them.

"Go, team!" Shelly said.

They raised their hands in the air, then set off on Operation Hail Mary.

# CHAPTER TEN

**KENZIE, SHELLY, TOMOKO, AND JULES HEADED OUT TO**
their separate classrooms.

All morning Kenzie tried passing notes to the other girls
in her class.

Do you like roller skating?
Circle one: Y/N

But the only person who saw her note was the teacher,
who it turned out wasn't interested in roller derby either.

During P.E. class, Kenzie ran through the field in the
middle of a soccer game to ask the players if any of them
skated, but before she could ask, the ball bounced hard into
her shin and she limped back off the field.

No one at lunch wanted to hear about the league, even when Kenzie offered to trade her cookie if they would let her sit and talk derby with them.

"What did you do to it?" one girl asked suspiciously as Kenzie waved the cookie in her face.

"Nothing!" Kenzie said. "Just eat it!"

The girl turned back to her table. Kenzie sighed. None of her Hail Marys were working.

She found Shelly and Jules at a corner lunch table.

"Any luck?" she asked.

Shelly shook her head. "It's really last minute," she said. "Everyone seems to have plans this weekend."

"Heck, even I had plans with drama club," Jules said.

Kenzie and Shelly raised their eyebrows.

"I'm not going," Jules said defensively. "I'll be at derby with you guys. All I'm saying is . . . I'm on the team and I had plans!"

Shelly drummed her fingers on the table.

"What do you think they'll say if we only show up with four?" she asked.

Kenzie shrugged. "I don't think it will be good."

Tomoko sat at the table next to Kenzie. She buried her face in her arms.

"Ugh," she grumbled. "People don't want to do anything fun."

Jules held up her juice box. "You said it."

Kenzie scanned over the cafeteria as the other girls ate. Why was it so hard to find another skater? It seemed a lot easier to add beginners to the team. They found Tomoko right away at the park, and Jules stood out of the crowd with her sword fight.

*Wait*, Kenzie thought.

"I have an idea for our fifth member," she told the group.

"Who is it?" Tomoko asked.

"A skater?" Shelly asked hopefully.

Kenzie smiled. "Meet me in front of school after class gets out," she said. "And you'll see."

She stole a look at Jules, but Jules was poking at the blob of food on her plate. That was OK. Jules could be surprised too.

"Places, everyone!"

Miss Moss clapped her hands from the front row of the auditorium.

Kenzie held the door behind her so it would close without making a sound. She snuck into one of the back rows and waited as the lights dimmed down. Shoes scuffled across the stage. A spotlight rose in the center over the same kid who had broken up the sword fight in the lunchroom. He stood next to two other boys.

"By my head, here come the Capulets."

"By my heel, I care not."

Another group of kids charged onto the stage. Near the back of the group was the girl with the long, shiny hair. She held a fake sword out. Kenzie's eyes widened. She blinked and suddenly she could see the girl in the center of the derby rink, skating and sword fighting alongside Jules. Jules was a little rowdier, sure, but

this girl was just as tough. She flourished her sword in the air and did a quick backspin on her skates.

Kenzie could see it so clearly in her mind. *This* was the girl for their team.

"Away!"

The skates vanished in Kenzie's head as the girl exited offstage. Kenzie slunk out of her seat and made her way to a section of curtain hidden in shadow. She pushed past the heavy velvet fabric.

Going from the auditorium to backstage was like flipping a switch. Everything went from dark and hushed to bright and animated. Kids were doing makeup on each other, putting on and taking off coats and vests, and practicing lines from their scripts. Kenzie waded through the whispering clusters of kids until she found the girl sitting in the far back corner. Her knees were tucked carefully up to her chin. The fake sword lay beside her.

"Hey," Kenzie said. She knelt in front of the girl. "I'm Kenzie. You were in the sword fight in the lunchroom, right?"

The girl looked up from her script. "Yes," she said timidly. "I'm Camila."

"You were great!" Kenzie said. She sat down in front of Camila and clasped her hands the way her dad did whenever he was about to launch into one of his stories.

"So I know you're in this play," Kenzie said. "And you're really good," she added. "But I'm on this roller derby team and we need another member, and I was thinking that since you're so good at fighting and stuff, you'd be perfect."

Camila tucked her hair behind one ear. "Well, I don't like actual fighting."

"Right," Kenzie said. She waved her hands. "Of course not. Just the play-fighting thing."

"What is roller derby?" Camila asked. "Is it like a play?"

Kenzie paused. She remembered getting upset when Shelly had told Tomoko that derby was like basketball.

"Sort of," Kenzie said. "Derby's a little like a play. There's five of us and we put on these uniforms—which are a lot like costumes, actually. And people cheer while we skate around a track."

Camila leaned forward. "I like costumes," she said. "But I don't know how to skate."

"Oh," Kenzie said, frowning. She had promised Shelly they would find a skater to finish the team. But now they only had one day to practice before the league began. And they needed a fifth person.

"That's OK," Kenzie told Camila. "The others don't really know either. We can practice tomorrow after school."

"Tomorrow?" Camila said. "That's really soon. What if I don't know how to skate by then either?"

Kenzie smiled. "It takes a while to really learn skating," she said. "Even I'm still learning. I fall all the time."

Kenzie was trying to help Camila get excited about derby, but she seemed to keep saying the wrong things.

"You *fall*?" Camila asked. Her eyes grew wide.

"But we wear pads and stuff, to not get hurt," Kenzie said quickly. She needed to show Camila that derby wasn't about getting beaten up; it was about being tough and having fun.

Kenzie pointed to the sword next to Camila. "You know how you have to use this in the play?"

Camila nodded. "For fight choreography," she said. "That's when we plan out moves for a pretend fight."

"Perfect!" Kenzie said. "Roller derby's a lot like fight choreography. We get to perform for crowds of people. And we train to make sure we don't really hurt ourselves."

Camila gathered her script to her.

"Is derby a . . . a sport?" she asked.

Kenzie chewed her lip. She couldn't just lie to Camila. That wouldn't be fair.

"Yes," Kenzie said.

Camila swallowed. "My dad really wants me to try sports. And my part in the play is really small." She looked at her script again.

"OK," she said. "I'll do it." She smiled to herself. "My dad will be so excited."

Kenzie gave a huge sigh of relief.

"You'll be great," Kenzie said. "And everyone will be cheering for you, not just your dad. Meet me after school tomorrow, and we'll get started. I can introduce you to the other girls. Well, you already know Jules."

Camila's face fell. "Jules is on the team?"

Kenzie nodded. "Yeah. She just joined."

"But . . . she doesn't listen to Miss Moss's fight choreography," Camila said. "It's really hard to have scenes with her."

"That's OK," Kenzie said. "Roller derby is different from performances. There's not one thing to do, like in a play. Derby's a sport, remember?"

"Oh. Right," Camila said uncertainly.

Kenzie gave a thumbs-up.

"See you after school tomorrow. Front steps!"

"OK," Camila said. She gave a thumbs-up back.

Kenzie wore a huge grin as she walked past the prop tables and costume racks. She emerged into the hall and jogged to the front of the school. As Kenzie pushed the doors open, she felt like she was finally coming up for air. She had done it. She had finished the team.

"I found her!" she cried. "I got our last member!"

Shelly, Tomoko, and Jules turned from the steps.

"Who is it?" Tomoko asked.

"Camila," Kenzie said.

Jules's eyebrows shot halfway up her forehead.

"Camila from drama club?"

"Yep," Kenzie said. "We're going to teach her how to skate tomorrow!"

"Wait a second." Shelly grabbed Kenzie's arm and took her aside. "I thought we decided to find a *skater*."

Kenzie held out her palms.

"What was I supposed to do?" she said. "The league starts on Saturday! We need five players."

"But what about Bree?" Shelly asked.

Kenzie glared at her. "Camila's our fifth player."

Kenzie glanced at the others. Jules sucked on her teeth and shook her head. Tomoko looked questioningly at Shelly. The team was in dire need of a pep talk.

"Look, we're all coming to derby for different reasons," Kenzie said. "But the important thing is that we're all here. There are five of us now. And tomorrow afternoon, we're going to practice as a team and kick butt!"

Kenzie held her arm into the circle.

"Der-by, der-by, der-by," she chanted.

Jules put her arm in next. Then Tomoko. Shelly sighed and placed her hand on top.

"Derby!" the team said in unison.

Kenzie smiled and nudged Shelly's side. Maybe they didn't quite have a dream team, but they did have a team, which meant they were headed for the track.

# CHAPTER ELEVEN

**"LADIES AND GENTS, EARLOBES AND ICE CUBES,"** THE announcer sang out. "Introducing Austin's first junior roller derby league! Please welcome to the track our leading ladies, the Dynamic Duo: Kenzilla and Bomb Shell!"

Kenzie and Shelly skated to the center of the rink. They held hands and twisted in circles, spinning faster and faster until they turned into a human cyclone, ready to take out their rivals on the track.

"Woo!"

The crowd went wild. They brought out their BOMB SHELL banners and waved their KENZILLA signs. Some of the little kids roared like they were Kenzilla monsters.

"And here's their superstar team: Tomoko, Jules, and Camila!"

Kenzie and Shelly stopped spinning and gestured toward the entrance. Tomoko made a perfect backflip onto the rink and tossed her basketball toward the bleachers. Jules sliced the air with her sword. Camila blew kisses to her fans as she skated close behind the others.

"They're ready to take on the competition," the announcer said. "As long as they pay attention. Hello? Anyone there? Kenzie, are you listening to me?"

Shelly snapped her fingers in front of Kenzie's face. Kenzie jolted upright.

"What?" she asked.

"Man," Shelly said, "you really check out sometimes. I was asking if you knew Camila's shoe size. For the skate rentals."

Kenzie shook her head. "Why would I know her shoe size?" she asked.

"Well, you're the one who got her for the team," Shelly said. "You think she's still coming?"

Kenzie looked at the school doors over her shoulder. It felt like the bell had rung ages ago. *Was* Camila still coming?

Tomoko rummaged through her backpack. Jules had plucked a blade of grass and was using it as a whistle.

"Hey, Jules?" Kenzie asked.

*Ffftttt!*

Jules looked up. "Yeah?"

"Was there rehearsal today? After school?"

Jules shrugged. "I dropped out," she said. "But I think so, yeah."

Kenzie buried her face in her hands. It seemed like the Hail Mary was a total bust.

"Hey," a soft voice said. Camila stood at the top of the steps.

Kenzie and Shelly jumped up together.

"Hi!" Kenzie said. "Ready for practice?"

Camila smoothed her shirt.

"Um. OK," she said. "I mean, I'm ready to leave. But I still haven't learned to skate."

Kenzie laughed. "That's what we're doing right now," she said. "Don't worry!"

Jules ran up the steps and linked her arm through Camila's.

"We can do our sword fight on wheels!"

Camila winced. Kenzie smiled encouragingly and came to Camila's other side.

"We'll start with regular skating," Kenzie said. She walked ahead with Camila and Jules, trying not to notice Shelly and Tomoko walking together behind her.

The girls popped into the roller derby warehouse. A woman sat behind the front desk reading a comic book.

"Is Wreck-the-Holls around?" Kenzie asked.

The woman hitched her thumb over her shoulder.

"Who's Wreck-the-Holls?" Tomoko asked.

"Ms. E.," Shelly whispered. "Kenzie's mom."

The girls found Kenzie's mom and the rest of the Hazel Nuts team skating laps on the main track. Kenzie's mom swiveled and stopped in front of Kenzie.

"Skate time?" she asked.

Kenzie nodded. Her mom led the group to the rental counter.

"All right, ladies. You can practice on the court behind the building. Take helmets and pads along with skates. Your skate size is your shoe size. And remember to be careful."

Kenzie, Shelly, Tomoko, and Jules all nodded. But Camila raised her hand.

"What do we have to be careful about?" she asked.

"Falling correctly," Kenzie's mom said. "The skates are plenty sturdy. But they're heavy, and if you land wrong you could get hurt. Kenzie and Shelly will show you ladies how to fall."

Camila's chin quivered.

"But I thought this was like fight choreography," she said. "You're not supposed to get hurt in fight choreography."

Shelly turned to Kenzie and raised an eyebrow.

"You don't get hurt if you do things right," Kenzie said. "I'll show you how to use your knee pads."

Kenzie swung her skates over her shoulder. She grabbed the bundle of elbow and knee pads from the counter and turned for the side door.

Shelly quickly caught up to her.

"Hey," Shelly said. "What was that?"

"What was what?" Kenzie asked.

"Why does Camila think roller derby is like fight choreography?"

Kenzie shrugged. "I have no idea," she said. "I mean . . . I might have said that derby was a *teensy* bit like the sword fighting she and Jules did in the cafeteria. I guess that's all she needed to know."

"Huh," Shelly said. "Well, maybe we should warn her that it will be really different."

"She'll find out in a couple of minutes," Kenzie said. "Come on, we're wasting practice time."

Kenzie dumped the padding next to a bench and sat down to change into her skates. Jules flew out of the door a minute later, followed by Tomoko. Camila emerged last. She was carrying her skates like they might bite her. Shelly turned to Kenzie, but Kenzie pretended to be busy tying her own skates.

"OK, guys," Kenzie said. "Make sure your laces are good and tight."

Jules stretched her laces taut as she yanked them over and under each loop.

"They're so tight, they might break my foot!" she said proudly.

"Don't cut off circulation," Shelly said. "The point is not to let them get loose."

"Oh, they won't," Jules assured her.

Tomoko wrapped her laces around her ankle and knotted them in the front.

"Whoa," Shelly said, "it took me months before I figured out how to tie them like that."

Tomoko blushed. "I was watching you guys," she said.

Kenzie buckled her helmet and stood up. She clapped

her hands the way Miss Moss had done at rehearsal. "Fasten your elbow pads and hustle to the court. Places!"

"These are really heavy," Camila said. She lifted a foot, then let it clack onto the ground.

"You get used to it," Kenzie said. "Your feet will slide more than walk anyway."

Camila frowned and tied her laces into a neat bow.

"You'll have to tie them a lot tighter than that," Shelly said. "Or the skates will fly off your feet."

"They will?" Camila asked. She looked down at her skates in horror.

"Leave her alone," Kenzie said. "You're scaring her!"

Shelly threw her hands up. "I'm trying to help!"

Tomoko pushed off from the bench.

"Whoa," she said. She wobbled her arms a moment, then held them out like she was walking on a tightrope. She kicked one of her legs and propelled herself forward.

"That's great!" Shelly said. "Make sure your legs go out to the side, not right behind you."

"OK," Tomoko said. She steadied herself and bent her knees, then rolled one skate out, then the other. Kenzie was impressed that Tomoko hadn't fallen right off the bat. Maybe they really would have a superstar team after all.

"Hi-yah!" Jules yelled.

She jumped up on her skates, then collapsed in a jumbled heap. Before anyone could help her, Jules pushed herself back up to standing. She reached out toward Tomoko and lunged again.

"Hi-yah!"

Kenzie watched as Jules went down like a stick building that had been blown over by the big bad wolf. Kenzie's cheeks flushed.

"I can't fall like that!" Camila said. "I bruise easily."

"That's OK," Shelly said. "Bruises are pretty normal here."

Camila shot a bewildered look at Kenzie. She kept a death grip on the bench as she stood up.

"Try letting go," Shelly said.

Camila froze. Her hand was firmly wrapped around the back of the bench. She whimpered and sat back down.

"I can't!" she cried.

Kenzie gave a long and low sigh.

"Well, that's just great," Shelly said, rolling her eyes. "We'll knock 'em dead tomorrow."

# CHAPTER TWELVE

**AN UNUSUAL CHILL HOVERED OVER AUSTIN THE NEXT** morning. Kenzie pressed a hand to her window, feeling the cold seep into her fingers. It was the kind of morning that made her want to crawl back under the blankets, or get a steamed milk at her favorite coffee shop with her dad.

But it wasn't time for blanket nests or hazelnut steamers.

It was time for derby.

Kenzie threw on her jacket. She stuffed her extra-thick derby socks and a water bottle into her bag.

"Greetings and salutations!" Verona said at the table. She leaned close to Kenzie and whispered: "That means 'good luck.'"

"Thanks," Kenzie said. After the practice they had had yesterday, their team needed all the luck they could get.

As Kenzie and her mom rounded the corner to the warehouse, Kenzie saw Shelly and Tomoko already waiting. Kenzie clutched her bag close to her. Jules jumped out from a red pickup truck. Camila slunk out of a shiny black car and waved toward the window.

Kenzie's mom unlocked the side door of the building.

"Fifteen minutes," she said to the girls. "Then the main doors open."

Kenzie and the others nodded. Fifteen minutes was better than nothing. By the time practice ended yesterday, the most Kenzie and Shelly were able to do was pry Camila off the bench. They still had to go over all the regular derby moves.

"OK," Kenzie said once the girls had on their skates. "Let's get out there."

Jules and Tomoko followed Shelly onto the track. Kenzie led Camila behind the group.

"I need the railing!" Camila yelled.

"Use my arm. I'm right here," Kenzie said. She helped Camila to where the others were lined up.

"So, Tomoko's already got the hang of this," Shelly said.

"But the way you move forward is by pushing your legs out to the side. Left, right."

"Left, right," Jules echoed. She kicked a leg out and, this time, she didn't immediately topple over.

"Exactly!" Shelly said. "You don't want to push your toe into the ground, because that's where your brake is, so you'll end up stomping instead of skating."

"How do we brake?" Tomoko asked.

"You can plow stop, which is when you angle your feet in to slow down. Or . . ." Shelly looked at Kenzie.

Kenzie sighed. "Derby players usually pivot so they're skating backward, then they use the toe brake."

Camila's lip trembled. "We're supposed to spin around in these things?"

"Spin like this!" Jules said. She whipped her shoulder around and fell to the floor.

Kenzie could see the hope draining out of Shelly's face.

"Let's try some blocking moves," Kenzie said. "Jules and Camila, blocking is a lot like sword fighting, so you two will be great. Whenever you're skating forward, you keep your knees bent and elbows out. Like this, see? That makes it hard for the jammer to weave through."

"How was that again?" Tomoko asked. She bent her knees and arms.

"Oh," Kenzie said. She waved Tomoko off. "You don't have to learn this part since you'll be our jammer."

"I thought you were the jammer," Tomoko murmured. "That's what Shelly said."

Kenzie froze with her elbows out. She turned to Shelly.

"What?"

Shelly shrugged. "I figured one of us needed to be jammer," she said, "since we're the only two who have actually practiced derby."

Kenzie could hardly believe what she was hearing. Shelly was changing around the team now, and she hadn't even asked Kenzie first?

"But what about our classic M&M moves?" Kenzie asked.

"Shelly showed me some moves at the park last night," Tomoko said. "After we left the warehouse."

Kenzie stared hard back and forth between Shelly and Tomoko. Her jaw was set tight. The Dynamic Duo wasn't crumbling after all, she realized.

Kenzie just wasn't a part of it anymore.

"Kenzilla, wait!" Shelly said.

Kenzie didn't listen. She turned away from the others and stomped off the track. Just as she sat down on the bench, the front warehouse doors peeled open. Kenzie prepared herself for the usual burst of kids that flew in during Free Skate. Instead, she was met with a steady line of girls in sweatshirts and leggings. Some of the girls went to the rentals counter. Some swung their bags onto the ground and began taking out their own skates.

One group of skaters sat on the other side of the rink across from Kenzie. All five girls wore matching shirts with cherries on the front. No one chatted or whispered or laughed as they strapped on their skates and buckled their helmets.

"Formation!" one of the girls called when they had finished gearing up.

The entire group slid onto the track, bending low and gathering speed as they took a lap together. Camila ducked as they flew by.

"Stances!" another girl ordered.

The group formed a line side by side. They crouched their shoulders in. The tallest girl of the group snarled as her fists went in front of her.

Kenzie swallowed the lump in her throat. The kids at Free Skate could be annoying, but these derby players were straight-up scary. Plus, they looked way older than fifth graders. Kenzie suddenly remembered the poster for the league announcement.

### GIRLS AGES 10–14

"Shoot," she whispered. These girls were definitely closer to fourteen.

Not far away on the track, Camila clomped like a zombie in her skates. Jules was somehow knocking herself down. And Shelly was still busy helping Tomoko. Kenzie shook her head. She tightened the straps on her knee pads, pulling until the bands dug into her skin.

"You OK?"

Kenzie looked up. Mambo Rambo stood in front of her carrying a clipboard.

Mambo hovered over Kenzie's knees.

"I think you have those a little too tight. They might cut off—"

"Circulation," Kenzie said. She pulled the knee pads loose. "I know, I know."

Mambo squinted at Kenzie for a moment. She glanced over at the others, where Jules was careening toward Camila and Shelly had linked her arm around Tomoko's.

"Hmm. Looks like things are a-changin'."

Kenzie waited for her to say something else, but Mambo simply tapped on her clipboard and rolled away. Kenzie took a deep breath.

"Be ready," she told herself. "Pivot forward. Roll with the punches."

She stared at her hands. She felt more like throwing a punch than rolling with one. The team on the track wasn't what she had imagined at all. So many things were going wrong. Tomoko and Jules weren't derby stars. Camila was afraid of even standing in skates. Shelly seemed further away than ever. And Kenzie wasn't ready to be the team's jammer. She was barely ready for the league as a blocker!

Kenzie wrung her hands. The splinter pain was back. It pulsed through her.

There was something else wrong. Something Kenzie didn't want to admit in her head, let alone out loud.

As she sat alone on the bleachers, Kenzie thought about the evening in the park. She pictured the way Bree had swerved around the corner on her skateboard. She remembered the warm, fluttery feeling she got in her arms when they were talking. Shelly was right, Kenzie realized. Bree would have made a great skater.

She wished Bree were a part of the team.

# CHAPTER THIRTEEN

**THE WHISTLE BLEW. ALL THE RUMBLING AND CHATTER IN**
the warehouse came to a halt.

"Welcome to junior roller derby!" Mambo called out. "I
need everyone over here for opening announcements."

Shelly and Tomoko skated over together. Kenzie tried not

to look at either of them. She watched as Jules and Camila stumbled off the track. Camila's legs were stiff and she looked a lot like a robot, but at least she wasn't holding on to the railing anymore.

Everyone gathered along the bleachers.

"It's great to see so many new faces," Mambo Rambo said, "as well as some faces I already know." She stole a quick look at Kenzie and Shelly, but Kenzie hardly felt like smiling. Her heart was lodged in her throat.

"As you may know from our posters or from the website, the junior league initially wanted players to try out on their own. My fellow coaches and I have prepared a series of games, warm-ups, and exercises to see who might be ready to join the league this season. But there are also a small number of players who wanted to join as teams. For those tryouts, we've decided to have those teams play a scrimmage against each other."

Someone in the crowd gasped.

"Scrimmages already?" another person said.

Camila leaned over Kenzie's shoulder. "You didn't say we had to try out!" she whispered.

"We'll be fine," Kenzie whispered back. "Don't worry."

But even Kenzie wasn't totally convinced. She had sort of forgotten about the tryout part of derby league until now. Some of the teams looked really good. Would Kenzie and the other girls even stand a chance?

Mambo tapped her clipboard.

"If you don't know the rules of derby yet," she said, "you're not alone. I'm going to explain how a scrimmage works, and I want everyone to pay attention."

Jules squirmed. Tomoko sat up tall.

"First," Mambo said. "In derby, a game is called a bout. Bouts are made up of two thirty-minute periods. During a playing period, the teams race in short sprints that we call jams. Yes?"

"Why don't they call derby games a jam?" one girl asked.

"Because there are a lot of jams per bout," Mambo said. "A jam is a race between two teams, and it's not more than a loop or two around the track. Jams only last two minutes.

"Now today, our teams aren't going to play a full bout," Mambo continued. "Instead, the scrimmage will be a total of six jams, with one break in the middle."

"How do you jam?" another girl asked.

"It's pretty simple," Mambo said. "The four blockers from each team line up in one area, and the two jammers—the main racers—set up on the jammer line behind the blockers. The blockers are called a pack, and it's the jammer's job to break through the pack and get out in front. With me so far?"

A bunch of wide-eyed faces nodded.

"Good. The first jammer to break out is the lead jammer, which means they can call off the jam whenever they want. So say Kenzilla breaks out first, but then falls—"

Someone in the crowd laughed. Kenzie's cheeks turned red.

"She can touch her hip and just like that"—Mambo snapped her fingers—"the jam's over before either team can score. But of course, the lead jammer doesn't want to have to call the jam off. The jammer wants to come back around the loop and break through the pack a second time. This time, every blocker from the opposite team a jammer passes is a point. Points aren't easy in derby, so it's a big deal to make it back around. Both jammers can score, but only the lead jammer can end the jam early."

Mambo peeked over her clipboard. Uneasy looks were traded across the crowd. Some of the girls had their hair twisted in their fingers.

"Anyway," Mambo said, "there are more rules than that, but I'll stop there so we can get started. We have four teams trying out. The first scrimmage will be . . ."

Kenzie crossed her fingers tight.

*Please please please don't put us against the good team,* she thought.

". . . the Holy Molies versus the Secret Agents."

Kenzie looked around. Two other groups of girls sat up

straight and stared at one another. None of the girls wearing cherry shirts moved. That had to mean . . .

"And our second game will be the Cherry Pits versus the . . ." Mambo paused and eyed Kenzie. Kenzie hunched her head down. Maybe if she didn't give a team name, this would all fade away like one of her daydreams.

"We're the Kenzillas!" Shelly called out.

Mambo smiled. "OK, the Cherry Pits versus the Kenzillas."

Now the group in matching shirts started to shift and whisper at one another. So they were the Cherry Pits. And they were about to cream Kenzie and the others right out of their skates.

Perfect.

Mambo blew the whistle and the first teams hustled to the track. Eight blockers huddled in one section, with the two jammers a few yards behind them. The jammers looked so alone. Kenzie shivered. She never imagined having to be the main person for her team. That was a lot of pressure.

Shelly rested her chin on Kenzie's shoulder. She made a puppy dog face.

"You'll be a great jammer," Shelly whispered. "Out of the two of us, you're way faster."

Kenzie turned around. "Is that why you kicked me out of the Dynamic Duo?"

Shelly sat back. "What?"

"I saw you show Tomoko our secret handshake."

"We both decided that," Shelly whispered. "She needed a friend."

"We were *supposed* to find her another friend," Kenzie hissed. "That's why I got Jules."

"Oh." Shelly stared down at the floor. "Well, I want to be friends with everyone."

Kenzie's heart sank. Having lots of friends didn't *seem* like the worst thing in the world. But what if it meant no more Duo . . . ever?

"First jam," Mambo called. "Positions. Pack—go!"

Kenzie turned away from Shelly and faced the track. She watched as the blockers lumbered forward.

"Jammers—go!"

The two girls on the jammer line charged into the group.

Kenzie tried to picture herself as a jammer, breaking through the pack and scoring a million points. But in real life, getting by the blockers seemed impossible. Kenzie couldn't figure out how anyone was supposed to pass that many people without being flung into the crowd.

One jammer took a hip check and fell onto her knees. The other jammer nudged her way out of the pack. She pumped her arms and skated hard to loop around again. She passed one blocker before she tripped and fell over.

Mambo held up a finger.

"Points: one to zero. Second jam."

The girls got back into position.

The more Kenzie watched each jam unfold, the more nervous she got about their own scrimmage. The jammer had to be lightning fast and super tough. Kenzie would hardly have time to be sad about missing out on the Dynamic Duo moves. She was going to be plenty busy staying alive on the track.

Soon the scrimmage bout was over. Both teams had fallen a lot, but the score wasn't very close: five to zero. Kenzie hoped she would score at least one point for her team, especially since Shelly named them the "Kenzillas." Kenzie's cheeks flushed as she imagined falling behind on every lap. What if she didn't get ahead, even once? What if the jammer from the Cherry Pits ran right over her?

Kenzie cringed. She needed to get this scrimmage over with before her imagination kept her from stepping on the track at all.

After Mambo called the end of the last jam, she and the two other coaches huddled together on the top row of bleachers. They murmured to one another, then made a bunch of scribbles up and down their clipboards. Kenzie closed her eyes and clutched her knees to keep them from trembling. She felt a hand over hers. She wished Shelly would leave her alone.

"Hey."

Kenzie opened her eyes. The hand wasn't Shelly's. It was Tomoko's.

"You'll be great," Tomoko told her. "You're such a good skater. And we'll be there to help you get through the pack. Promise."

For the first time since they arrived at the warehouse that morning, Kenzie's chest felt a tiny bit lighter.

"Thanks," she said.

"OK, ladies," Mambo said. She finished her last scribble with a flourish, then set her clipboard facedown.

"Second scrimmage. Kenzillas and Cherry Pits, let's go!"

# CHAPTER FOURTEEN

**TOMOKO PULLED KENZIE UP TO STANDING. SHELLY AND** Jules checked each other's gear.

"Camila?" Jules asked. "Are you OK?"

Camila's usually warm olive skin had gone pale. Even the shiny curls in her hair seemed deflated. Kenzie reached for a helmet and placed it over Camila's head.

"You'll be fine," Kenzie said. "I promise. Helmets and knee pads make it OK to fall."

Camila jerked her chin back. "But I don't want to fall."

"Falling is great!" Jules said.

"Just focus on skating," Shelly said. "Tomoko and Jules and I will work on blocking. Kenzie, we'll try to clear some spaces for you. Anything you want us to do?"

Kenzie sighed. "Are you and Tomoko going to use our Dynamic Duo moves?"

"What Dynamic Duo moves?" Tomoko asked. "Shelly only showed me how to pivot and hip check."

Kenzie turned to Shelly. "Really?"

"The Duo moves are for you and me," Shelly said. "We'll break them out at another game."

Kenzie squeezed Shelly's hand. "If we can still get in," she said.

"Oh, we're getting in," Jules said. She clipped her helmet and put her hand into the circle.

"Heck yes we are!" Tomoko said. She threw her hand in next.

Kenzie and Shelly looked at each other. Kenzie felt a smile creeping on.

"Let's win this, then," she said.

"Camila?" Shelly asked. "Come on! Team chant."

Camila sniffled as she stuck her hand in.

"Gooooo, Kenzillas!"

The girls rolled onto the track. The Cherry Pits were already in place. Kenzie skated behind the blockers, stopping next to a girl who was a whole head taller than her. Kenzie gulped. Maybe being short would help her squeeze through the pack, but how was she supposed to catch up

with the other jammer in the first place? Her legs were twice as long as Kenzie's!

Tomoko smiled at Kenzie, then turned to the front. Someone in the main group let out a high-pitched squeak. Kenzie guessed it was Camila.

"Pack—ready," Mambo said.

The eight girls in front crouched low. Kenzie took a deep breath. This was it. Her first real derby game.

"Pack—go!"

The blockers scrambled into motion. Kenzie balled her fists and closed her eyes. Whenever she *imagined* playing derby, she always saw hundreds of faces in the crowd. She could read the words on the signs as they waved. She could hear her name being chanted.

But in real life, being on the derby track was way different. Even if there had been a huge crowd, Kenzie never would have heard or saw them. Instead, all Kenzie could hear was her heart thumping in her chest and her breath as it raced in and out of her mouth. All she could see was a flurry of wheels on the track.

"Jammers—go!"

Kenzie's eyes shot open. She pumped her arms and kicked her skates out to the side.

*Don't fall*, she told herself. *Don't fall. Don't fall. Don't fall.*

Kenzie and the other jammer zoomed forward. In just a few strides, the other girl slid in front. Kenzie could only see the backs of her skates as she worked to catch up to the pack. Kenzie

groaned. Her worst fears were coming true. She wouldn't even score one point by the time the scrimmage was over.

"Incoming!"

Shelly and Tomoko suddenly broke from the other blockers and pinned the Cherry Pits jammer behind them. The jammer swerved one way and then another, but Tomoko and Shelly would not let her through. Kenzie watched as a gap opened between two other girls.

"Go! Go!" Tomoko yelled.

Kenzie put her head down and barreled forward. She caught up to the pack and slipped between the Cherry Pits blockers.

"Lead," Mambo called as Kenzie broke out in front.

A jolt of energy ran through Kenzie's veins. She was the

lead jammer! She could end the jam right now, before the other team had time to score. Or maybe she could earn some points herself!

Kenzie bent her knees as she skated around a curve. She could hear the other jammer's skates roaring behind her. She had to score fast, then end the jam before the Cherry Pits could get any points. She ducked under one blocker's arm.

*Point!*

Shelly looked over her shoulder. She leaned into another blocker and cleared a path. Kenzie sailed past two more Cherry Pit blockers as the other jammer approached the pack.

*Point! Point!*

Kenzie touched her hip.

"End jam!" Mambo called. She blew the whistle. "Kenzillas: three. Cherry Pits: one."

"Woo!" Shelly turned and gave Kenzie a high five. "Three points. You are on fire!"

"I didn't fall!" Jules yelled.

Tomoko put a hand on Jules's shoulder. "We're so proud," she said with a grin.

The other girls turned to Camila. "Camila, you all right?"

Camila looked frozen. She made a slight bob with her head. Jules tapped Camila's fist.

"You're doing awesome!" she said.

"Jam two," Mambo yelled. "Positions."

Mambo blew the whistle once, then twice as she pointed at the jammers. Right away, the other girl got ahead again.

*That's OK*, Kenzie thought. *I'll wait for my team to block her, then look for the gap.*

The jammer came up right behind Jules. Together, Tomoko and Jules swooped to the side to keep her from passing. Kenzie took a breath and hurtled forward. She passed the other jammer. The gap wasn't as clear this time. Kenzie would have to weave between players if she was going to come out as lead jammer. Camila wobbled back and forth as she skated at the front of the group, blocking Kenzie's way.

"Hey," Kenzie called. "Head right!"

Camila held her arms out wide.

"I can't fall!" she cried

"Camila, move!" Shelly said.

Kenzie hung back. She didn't want to slam into her own teammate. She felt something brush her arm. The Cherry Pits jammer had gotten by Tomoko and Jules.

"Lead," Mambo said.

*No,* Kenzie thought.

She raced through the pack, dipping out of Camila's reach. The two jammers whipped around the loop. The Cherry Pits jammer was flying. Kenzie needed to score some points before the other girl called off the jam. She dove through the players.

"End jam," Mambo said. "Cherry Pits: four. Kenzillas: two."

The girls returned to the pack line.

"Five to five," Tomoko said, frowning. "We're tied now."

"We still have another jam before halftime," Shelly said.

Jules turned to Camila. "What was that? You blocked your own teammate!"

Camila's eyes were glossy. "I wasn't trying to do anything," she said. "I just don't want to fall!"

Shelly sighed. Kenzie looked away. She never should have made Camila join the team. But it was too late to undo it now.

Mambo's booming voice rose above the others.

"Jam three!"

The whistle blew twice.

Kenzie and the other jammer took off. Kenzie put every bit of energy she had into keeping up this time. The wheels on her skates barely touched the track. Both jammers reached the pack at the same exact moment.

Kenzie grinned. She saw a gap open in front of her. She just had to make sure she got to it first.

"Look out!" someone called.

*WHAM!*

Kenzie didn't even turn her head before she landed smack on the floor. Jules was lying right beside her. Jules blinked at Kenzie and scrambled to her feet. She rushed to pull Kenzie up after her.

"I—I didn't mean to hit you," Jules said, stuttering. "I was trying to hip check!"

Kenzie nodded. There was no time to talk. The other

jammer was far ahead of the pack and circling for another lap. Kenzie rushed after her, but she was only halfway around the track when Mambo blew her whistle.

"End jam," she called. "Cherry Pits: four, Kenzillas: zero. Total half score is nine to five. Ten minutes of halftime, then positions for jam four."

The whirlwind of skates slowed to a stop.

Kenzie caught her breath and glanced over her team. Camila was already off the track. Shelly stood dejected in place. Tomoko stared at her laces. Even Jules had lost her bouncy energy.

It wasn't fair. They had worked so hard to get a group together, to come skate as a team on the track. Their chance to play derby was so close—they couldn't lose it now. They just couldn't.

Kenzie gritted her teeth. She had a plan. The Kenzillas were going to come back from halftime and *win*.

# CHAPTER FIFTEEN

THE TEAM SPRAWLED OUT ON THE SIDELINES. CAMILA huddled on the bench. Tomoko bent over her knees, massaging her ankles.

"Man, wearing these things will take some getting used to," she said.

"If we even make it into the league," Jules said. She tightened one of her elbows pads. "I probably ruined everything."

Shelly sighed and took a swig of her water bottle.

"You didn't ruin everything," Kenzie said. "It was a mistake. Mistakes happen all the time in derby."

"What are we supposed to do now, though?" Shelly asked. "I mean, you're fast, but you're not nearly as fast as the Cherry Pits jammer. No offense."

Kenzie dropped down on a knee and took off her wrist

guards. She grabbed her own water bottle, then Shelly's, then Tomoko's.

"What are you doing?" Shelly asked.

"I'm making a game play," Kenzie said. Her voice sounded stronger than she felt. "You're right," she told Shelly. "The other girl is faster than me. But we schooled them on the first jam. We can do that again. We just have to plan it."

"Maybe my plan is to stay on the sidelines," Jules said quietly.

Kenzie held her hand out.

"Give me your water bottle," she ordered. "You're a part of this too."

Jules straightened up. She handed her bottle to Kenzie.

"OK," Kenzie said. She put three of the water bottles together on the floor, then moved her own bottle behind them, the way the girls set up on the track. "You guys are up here, and I'm behind you when the whistle blows."

Shelly crouched down next to Kenzie. "Right."

"I need help with stopping the other jammer and finding an opening. Shelly and Tomoko, you guys did a really cool move on the first jam. What was that again?"

Shelly and Tomoko looked at each other.

"Well," Shelly said, "I tried to get in the jammer's way."

"And then I kept the other team's blocker from helping," Tomoko said.

"Great." Kenzie pointed at Jules. "Remember how you tackled me in the last jam?"

Jules dropped her head.

"I know, I know. I'm sorry."

"No, it was perfect," Kenzie said. She smiled. "Just aim for a Cherry Pits blocker. I only need one gap to get through, so if you can hip check right before I get to you, I'll be able to skate forward."

"Right," Jules said. She pumped her fist.

"And for Camila, I need you to . . . Camila? Hey, Camila!"

Camila was staring into space. Her shoulders were shaking.

"What?" she said, jerking her head.

"Hand me your water bottle," Kenzie said. "We're going to bounce back from this."

"Five minutes!" Mambo called from the top of the bleachers.

Camila stood up from the bench. She leaned toward her bag, arm outstretched. Suddenly her skates flew out from under her.

*Crash.*

"Oh no," Shelly whispered.

"Camila," Tomoko said, "are you OK?"

Camila was collapsed on the floor. She held her wrist close to her chest.

"Is it sprained?" Kenzie asked. She reached for Camila. "Let's see if you can turn it or not."

Camila pulled away. Her head sunk below her shoulders.

"I can't do this," she sobbed. "I've always wanted to be tough. And to like sports. And to look cool. But I can't. I'm not. I hate wearing skates and trying not to fall over. I hate it!"

The rest of the group went silent. Kenzie winced, waiting for Shelly's big "I told you so." But when Kenzie looked back at Shelly, she didn't see an angry face, or even an "I told you so" face. Instead, Shelly's eyes were soft.

Kenzie turned to Tomoko and Jules. Their foreheads were

both creased with worry. No one was mad, Kenzie realized. They were sad.

Camila buried her face in her hands. "My wrist hurts," she moaned. She looked up at Kenzie. "You said elbow pads and helmets keep us safe, but my ankles hurt. And my feet hurt. Everything hurts."

Kenzie blinked. She had been so surrounded with her mom's derby bouts and practices at Free Skate that she forgot that getting hurt in derby meant two different things. There was the bad hurt that came from falling wrong or slamming into the railing. But there was also the normal hurt from tying skates tight and giving hip checks. Derby wasn't for people who didn't like getting hurt at all.

Kenzie bent over and started unlacing one of Camila's skates. Tomoko crawled to the other skate and helped loosen Camila's foot out of it.

"Let's get Mambo over here," Shelly said. "She'll look at your wrist."

Camila nudged the skates away with her toe. "I . . . don't want to play either way," she said uneasily.

"That's OK," Jules said. "Right?"

"Right," Kenzie said. She sighed. "I'm sorry for making you play, Camila. I should have listened to you before."

Kenzie stepped onto the bleachers.

"Wait," Tomoko said. "What happens now?"

Kenzie shrugged. "Mambo will look at Camila's wrist."

"Yeah, but what about the bout? Do we really need five players? We can totally win with three blockers and a jammer."

"There has to be five," Shelly murmured.

Tomoko slouched over. Kenzie and Shelly nodded at each other. They didn't have to crawl into the M&M brain to know what they needed to do.

Jules patted Camila's shoulder. "Dude. Sometimes it's brave to back out."

Camila sniffed into her sleeve. She wiped her eyes. "R—really?"

Tomoko nodded.

"Better now than later," Shelly said. "For real."

"Maybe we can still try out on our own," Kenzie said encouragingly. "And then we might get put on the same team anyway. I'll ask Mambo."

She turned toward the main bleachers before her smile slid right off. They wouldn't all make it into the league on their own, Kenzie knew. It was too competitive. There were too many girls. The only chance the Kenzillas had had was as a team. And now their chance was gone.

Kenzie was upset. But not with Camila. It was her own fault for rushing Camila into derby in the first place. Because of her dumb Hail Mary, Shelly and Tomoko and Jules were about to kiss their derby dreams goodbye. Just as they were figuring out how to kick butt on the track.

Kenzie shook her head. Dreams or no dreams, they had to help Camila.

She had to tell Mambo the Kenzillas were out of the league.

# CHAPTER SIXTEEN

"ONE MINUTE!" MAMBO CALLED, HEADING DOWN THE steps.

Kenzie met her at the first row of bleachers.

"Hey, Mambo," she said. "There's been a change of plans."

Mambo raised an eyebrow. She looked over Kenzie's shoulder.

"Is everyone OK?" she asked.

"Well, that's the change," Kenzie said. "We have to—"

"Switch!" someone yelled.

Kenzie froze. The hairs on her arms stood on end. She turned and gazed at the crowd. She knew that voice. But where had it come from?

Suddenly, an opening formed in the middle of the other

skaters. Bree—*Bree!*—emerged and glided forward—*on roller skates!* She came to a smooth stop at the bottom of the bleachers.

"Reporting for duty," Bree said with a bow.

Kenzie's jaw hung open. She closed it quickly and coughed, then looked away. She hoped her cheeks weren't turning an intense shade of red—again.

"What's going on?" Mambo asked.

"Didn't you see?" Bree nodded

toward the bench with Shelly and the others. "One of the Kenzilla players got hurt. I'm the alternate."

Mambo peered over at Camila. "Hold on," she said. She made her way to the rest of the Kenzillas, leaving Kenzie and Bree standing together.

Kenzie stared at her neighbor. Bree must've been at tryouts all along, she realized. There were so many girls—it would have been impossible to see her in the crowd. But why did she want to join the team now? What about what Shelly had said at the park?

"Hey!"

Shelly skated next to Bree. "You upgraded!"

"My skateboard's at home," Bree said. "But I figured I'd try out roller derby. It would be nice to skate with some friends." She turned to Kenzie and gave a shy smile. "And maybe some *non-friends* too."

Kenzie blushed. She felt the jitters come rushing back into her stomach. But, this time, they didn't slosh around like liquid. They were light, like bubbles floating inside her. Looking at Bree in skates made Kenzie want to float. It made her want to do impossible things.

Shelly lunged forward and wrapped her arms around Bree.

"Thank you thank you thank you," she squealed.

Bree laughed and pressed Shelly back to standing.

"Don't mention it," she said.

Bree and Shelly skated to the bench as Mambo led Camila to the main bleachers. Tomoko and Jules stood and threw their arms over Bree's shoulders.

A voice kicked up in Kenzie's mind.

"Here she is, folks," the announcer said. "The coolness queen. The derby star who tears up the track in her sleep. The skater of your dreams—Bree!"

Kenzie shook her head. The announcer's words faded.

"Good luck!" Camila called. "Don't break a leg!"

Kenzie grinned and gave a thumbs-up to Camila, then skated to the group. As she looked across at her four team-mates, something clicked in Kenzie's mind. The team finally felt *whole*. It felt *real*.

Kenzie, Shelly, Bree, Tomoko, and Jules formed a huddle.

"One minute!" Mambo called.

"There's not enough time for a new plan," Shelly said.

"That's OK," Kenzie said. "I know what to do. Bree, you're the fastest on wheels, and you're way better at keeping your balance than me. You be jammer."

Bree nodded. "Got it."

"Perfect," Tomoko said. "Now Kenzie and Shelly can do their blocking moves on the other jammer, and Jules and I can clear a path for Bree. Sound good?"

Kenzie peered across the circle at Shelly. Shelly held out a fist.

"Dynamic Duo," she said.

Kenzie put her fist in.

"Trio!" Jules brought her hand in.

"Quartet!" Tomoko said, giggling.

"Cinco! . . . Or something," Bree added. "The Kenzillas!"

"Positions!" Mambo called out.

Kenzie was relieved to be standing next to her teammates this time. At first she felt bad that Bree was standing on the jammer line . . . until she remembered how much Bree liked to show off. Kenzie wanted to turn and look at her, just for a moment, but she had to focus on the jam.

"Banshee?" Shelly whispered.

Kenzie thought for a moment.

"Tiger," she whispered back.

Mambo blew the whistle. The blockers skated forward. Skating was completely different in the pack, Kenzie realized. She didn't have to go fast, but she had to be ready for the jammers to come up from behind like a surprise sneak attack. How would she know which jammer to block and which jammer to let through? Now Kenzie understood why Jules had accidentally slammed into her before.

"Zilla!" Kenzie heard over her right shoulder. That was Bree.

She heard the slick rolling wheels of a different player over her left shoulder. Kenzie and Shelly nodded at each other. The Dynamic Duo was ready.

"Rawr!!!"

Both Kenzie and Shelly turned in perfect unison. They curled their fingers into claws and growled at the Cherry Pits jammer.

"Augh!" the jammer cried. She stumbled back and wobbled on one leg.

Bree took the opening and zipped through the pack. By the time the Cherry Pits jammer was through, Bree was deep into her loop. Kenzie listened for the sound of Bree's skates versus the other girl's. Bree was the clack, clack, clack as she threw herself forward with each stride. When she came around again, Kenzie made sure to get out of the way. Bree whooshed right by her, but the other jammer wasn't far behind.

"End jam!" Mambo said. "Kenzillas: three, Cherry Pits: one."

"Wait a second." The Cherry Pits jammer swiveled to Mambo. She pointed at Kenzie and Shelly. "They jumped out at me! Isn't that a foul?"

"It is if there's contact," Mambo said. "But you were still a ways behind them."

The jammer turned and glared at Kenzie.

"Growling? Really? What are you—a Tasmanian daredevil or something?"

"Nope! We're the Kenzillas!" Shelly said, bouncing at Kenzie's side.

The girl rolled her eyes. "Yeah, well. You're lucky Coach likes you."

She skated back into place.

"Jam five," Mambo called. "Positions."

"We're catching up," Tomoko said excitedly as the girls returned to the pack.

"Let's switch things around," Kenzie said. "Maybe you and Shelly go for the jammer this time, and Jules and I will help Bree."

"Why?" Shelly asked.

Kenzie nodded her chin at the Cherry Pits jammer. "To show the other team that we're playing fair," she said. "We're not lucky. We're *earning* all these points."

"Yes, we are," Bree said.

Tomoko smiled. "OK, I'm in."

"Me too!" Shelly said.

Bree nodded and took her place on the jammer line.

Kenzie high-fived Jules and got in position.

It was time to show these Cherry Pits what a real hip check looked like.

# CHAPTER SEVENTEEN

**"JAM FIVE. PACK—GO!"**

The blockers took off in a frenzy.

Jules's skates flew out in every direction as she scrambled forward. Kenzie worked hard to skate next to her. It had been easy to stay close to Shelly. After years of practice, Kenzie knew everything about the way Shelly skated. But working with Jules was way different. Jules skated like she was bolting from her own shadow. Kenzie sped up and slowed down, trying to stick by Jules's side.

*Whirrrrrrrrrr.*

Kenzie and Jules glanced at each other. That was the sound the Cherry Pits jammer's skates made. For a moment Kenzie held her breath, worried the jammer would crash straight into her as she raced through the pack. But Shelly and Tomoko snapped into action; they spread out across the track and trapped the jammer behind them.

"Ugh!" the jammer cried.

Kenzie smiled.

*Clack-clack-clack.*

"That's our cue," Jules said.

Bree was coming fast. Kenzie and Jules tensed their arms. They needed to clear the way for their own jammer.

"Shift to one side," Kenzie told Jules. "Then release into the hip check."

"Like the swings," Jules said. "I remember!"

Two blockers from the Cherry Pits had turned to trap Bree the way Tomoko and Shelly were blocking the other jammer. But Kenzie and Jules were ready for them.

"Excuse ME!" Jules said, swinging her hips into one of the blockers. The girl lost her footing and stumbled to the side.

Kenzie hip checked into another blocker. Even one hit made her hip instantly sore. But it opened a small path for Bree.

Bree raced ahead of the pack. She was like lightning. Kenzie couldn't help staring as Bree flew around the track, the other jammer not far behind. Bree looked like she had been skating her whole life. How was she so good?

Kenzie swallowed and turned again to the pack. The group

was already bracing for the jammers to come around again. Kenzie spotted a Cherry Pits blocker waiting for Bree.

"Not today!" Kenzie sang.

She skated over and hip checked into the blocker. Bree zigzagged her way through the pack. Mambo blew the whistle.

"End jam. Kenzillas: four points, Cherry Pits: two points. Final jam positions."

"You guys, you guys, you guys." Tomoko was practically jumping from foot to foot as the girls gathered. "We're tied. *We* have twelve. *They* have twelve. We can do this. We can win!"

"Heck yeah we can!" Jules said. "Did you guys see how I landed that hip check? Blocker never saw it coming! Hit the ground and everything."

"I thought you hit the ground too," Shelly said.

"Yeah, but that's not the point," Jules said. "I helped Kenzie make a path for Bree, so I'm good."

"You are good," Kenzie said. "We're all doing really good."

"Bree especially," Shelly said.

Bree grinned. "So what do we want to do for the final jam?" she asked. "Same positions as before?"

"I'm sticking with hip checks!" Jules said.

"I . . . kind of want to hip check another blocker," Shelly admitted. She glanced at Kenzie. "Is that OK?"

"That would put Tomoko and me in charge of the Cherry Pits jammer," Kenzie said. She thought of the way the jammer glared at her earlier. She pictured the jammer's roller skates smacking into her shins.

Kenzie flinched. "No problem," she said meekly.

"Let's do this!" Bree said. The girls brought a fist bump to the middle of their circle.

Kenzie crouched next to Tomoko and took a deep breath in, then out. Her heart slowed in her chest. The first jam already seemed like years ago. All the nervousness she had had about playing derby in real life transformed into excitement for winning the scrimmage. She belonged in derby—the whole team did. They were so close to proving it to Mambo and the rest of the league.

As the final start whistle blew, Kenzie was determined to stay by Tomoko's side. Luckily, Tomoko was a lot more consistent than Jules. Kenzie could hardly believe that Tomoko was so new to skating. Shelly had called it: put Tomoko in skates and "wa-bam!" She was a natural.

Kenzie listened for the sounds of either jammer behind her, but the whirring and clacking were all mixed together.

Someone was coming up fast. Kenzie's breath hitched in her throat. Was it Bree or the other girl? The other jammer had gotten ahead every other time. Kenzie threw her arms out and spread herself across the track.

"Argh," Bree said as she ran into Kenzie's shoulder.

"Shoot!"

Kenzie tried to pull away, but as she leaned to one side of the track, the other jammer swept past. Bree grunted and took off after her.

"Lead jammer—Cherry Pits," Mambo called.

*Oh no*, Kenzie thought. If the other jammer was in front, that meant she could call off the jam whenever she liked. Bree would have to keep up for the whole lap.

Bree seemed to be thinking the exact same thing as Kenzie. She kept her elbows close at her sides as she lunged after the Cherry Pits jammer.

Kenzie got ready for the other jammer to come around again. If the jammer couldn't pass anyone, then she'd have to call the jam off, and the score would still be tied. It was the team's only chance.

*Whirrrrrrr.*

The jammer was heading straight for Kenzie.

Kenzie licked her lips and wiggled her fingers. She imagined herself as a huge wall made of thick steel that no one could ever, ever get past. Maybe Kenzie would end up blocking like Jules, and go down along with her opponent. But that would be OK, so long as they didn't lose points.

"Oof!"

The other jammer slammed into Kenzie's side. Kenzie's knees buckled. Tomoko glided over.

"I got her," Tomoko said.

But Kenzie couldn't find her balance. She was careening straight toward Tomoko.

"Look out!" she cried. Tomoko barely saw Kenzie coming before they collided and crumpled in a heap over the track.

The ground vibrated as the rest of the pack stampeded forward.

*Whirrrrrrrrr.*

Kenzie pulled her skates in close. She wasn't hurt, but she felt like throwing up. She watched as the other jammer passed by Shelly.

"End jam!" Mambo said. "Cherry Pits: three points, Kenzillas: two.

"Bout winners: Cherry Pits."

# CHAPTER EIGHTEEN

**KENZIE'S STOMACH SANK DOWN BELOW HER RIB CAGE.**

That was it.

All their hard work with building the team, then facing off against the Cherry Pits . . . and they had lost.

Mambo was gathering the Cherry Pits over to talk to the other coaches. Kenzie imagined them getting stickers with the word *Winner* placed right next to the cherries on their shirts. Or maybe they would get brand new special jerseys to wear for official roller derby practice.

As she watched the other team climb the bleachers, Kenzie didn't move from where she had fallen. She could feel Tomoko scrunched up behind her. Kenzie sighed. She was the one who took Tomoko down. She lost the points. Losing the final jam was all her fault. Her heart twisted inside her.

"You OK?" Shelly asked. She knelt next to Kenzie.

"I wish we wouldn't have been the Kenzillas," Kenzie said miserably. "It was bad luck. I'm the reason we lost."

"Hey, I fell too."

Kenzie turned. Tomoko pulled herself over to the girls.

"Of course you fell," Kenzie said. "I ran into you."

"And the other jammer ran into you!" Shelly said. "Derby is really tough, remember? It's not for everyone."

"It's for me," Jules said. She dropped down next to Kenzie. "Even though I accidentally tackled you."

"It's for me too." Bree did a running slide, wedging herself in between Kenzie and Jules. Her arm nestled against Kenzie's shoulder.

"I could've skated faster," Bree said. "We all did things wrong. We gave it our best shot."

"Yeah," Kenzie muttered. She stared down at her skates. "I just wish I hadn't fallen at the end."

"But we're supposed to fall. That's why we have these." Shelly nudged Kenzie's knee pads and smiled. "It's so we can get back up and keep skating."

"I'm down for that," Bree said.

"Me too," Tomoko and Jules said together.

Kenzie gave a half smile. Maybe she and Shelly wouldn't be playing in the league . . . but they did have a team to play with now.

"Though, you're right about one thing," Shelly said. "We shouldn't be the Kenzillas. We need a better name for the whole team."

"Ladies!"

The girls looked across the track. Mambo was waving both arms in the air like an airplane traffic controller.

"Hello, Earth to skaters. We're ready to chat with you now."

Kenzie slumped over. They already lost the scrimmage. Did they really need to hear all the things they did wrong?

"Come on," Jules said.

The girls lugged each other up, one by one. They skated as a pack toward the bleachers. Even if they didn't win, Kenzie had to admit that they looked pretty great skating together as a team. Their skates clomped up the metal stairs. They reached the top row, where the two other coaches were waiting with clipboards in front of them.

One of the coaches waved. "You ladies can call me Lo, short for Look Out!"

"And I'm Razzle Dazzle," the other coach said. "But I go by Raz."

Mambo took her seat next to the coaches and held her clipboard in front of her.

"As Kenzie's mom may have told you," Mambo started, "we weren't so sure about adding preformed teams to the league. Originally, Raz, Lo, and I wanted to help junior skaters determine positions. There's a lot that goes into a team. The players have to work together exceptionally well."

Kenzie's eyes slid to her feet again. She thought about when Jules tackled her, or when she ran into Tomoko, or when Camila hurt her wrist and had to leave. She winced.

"I have to admit, I didn't love the Kenzillas that first stepped onto the track," Lo said. She tapped the end of her pen on the clipboard. "The most important thing to conquer in derby is fear, and there was a lot of fear before that whistle blew."

The girls nodded.

"And if your alternate hadn't come along, we would have a lot more concerns," Raz said. She tilted her head at Bree, who—Kenzie nearly did a double take—blushed and smiled.

"But we're impressed with the way your team handled the challenges of the scrimmage," Mambo said. "Kenzie, you did a great job strategizing at halftime. And rather than stick to the same positions, we loved that you gave each other turns. We think you make a good team."

Kenzie sniffed. She could feel herself wanting to cry.

"Thanks for letting us try," she said.

"Try?" Mambo tilted her head. "We're trying to tell you, you girls are in. You did it."

"What?"

The teammates looked at one another.

"But . . . we lost," Tomoko said.

Raz smirked. "And who said you had to win to make the league?"

"Nobody, I guess," Shelly said. "But the other team was so good."

"The Cherry Pits are in too," Mambo said. "You can have a rematch once we get to bout season."

"Here." Lo took out a piece of paper from her clipboard and handed it to Bree. "Mambo, Raz, and I still need to form the other teams. Fill out as much information as you can on this sheet, then turn it in before you leave. You can finish the rest at practice."

*Practice!*

Mambo grabbed a stack of purple slips and handed them to each girl. "And these are for your parents to sign. Don't lose them. See y'all next weekend. Sound good?"

Kenzie's cheeks hurt from smiling so wide.

"Sounds good," she said.

The others nodded like bobbleheads. They scrambled down the steps after Bree to their duffel bags. Bree snagged a pen from her pack.

"OK," Bree said. "Looks like they want names, birthdays, cell phone numbers, parent info—the works." She clicked her pen and started filling out one section of the form. Next, she passed it to Tomoko, then on to Jules, then to Shelly.

Kenzie had just put on her shoes when the paper fluttered in her lap.

*Kenzie Ellington*, she wrote for her name.

*Kenzilla*, she wrote for her derby name.

"Hey," Kenzie said. "The rest of you still need derby names."

"I wouldn't know what to choose," Tomoko said shyly.

"That means we can brainstorm!" Shelly squealed. "Lo said we could finish filling this out next week. Anyone up for pizza and derby-dubbing?"

"Yeah!" Jules said.

"Wait." Bree pointed at the very top of the sheet. "We should probably fill the first line out, though. Before we turn this in."

Team name: _____

The girls looked at one another blankly. Then Shelly clapped her hands.

"I've got one," she said.

"What is it?" Tomoko asked.

Shelly turned to Kenzie. "Remember what the Cherry Pits jammer called us? After we growled at her?"

"Lucky?" Kenzie asked.

"No," Shelly said. "She called us Tasmanian daredevils. I think we should be the Daredevils! Daredevils are brave and strong . . . and yeah, maybe they take some pretty big risks. But they're awesome. And so are we!"

Kenzie looked at Shelly. She thought about the names they had come up with at the park earlier in the week. The M&Ms . . . the Scream Queens . . . none of those felt right anymore. It was impossible to add people to a Dynamic Duo. But as Kenzie sat between Jules and Bree, her skate laces tangled with Tomoko's, she realized that roller derby wasn't about the Dynamic Duo. It was about the team. Things were different now. Things were . . . better.

"It's perfect," Kenzie said. "We are so totally the Daredevils."

Shelly beamed and folded her arms proudly.

Bree wrote DAREDEVILS! at the top of the sheet.

"Pizza time!" Jules cried out.

"And maybe ice pops after," Shelly said.

"OK, but no Sour Birthdays for me," Tomoko said. "Bleh. Only you and Kenzie like that one."

The girls slung their bags over their shoulders. Kenzie handed in the info sheet while the others turned in their skates. The team clustered together as they left the warehouse. Bree's hand hung next to Kenzie's, their fingers tapping every few steps. Kenzie's skin glowed. She wondered what it would be like to hang out with Bree off the track.

"I'm so hungry I could eat a horse," Shelly said as they walked.

"I'm so hungry I could eat one of my shoes!" Jules added.

"I don't think anyone would ever be hungry enough to smell one of your shoes, let alone eat it," Tomoko said.

Bree pinched her nose. "I'm exactly hungry enough for pizza."

"Yeah," Jules said. "Lots and lots of pizza."

Kenzie laughed and nodded. She hoped the pizza place was ready for a bunch of ravenous Derby Daredevils.

# ACKNOWLEDGMENTS

This book was made possible thanks to three extraordinary people. Thank you to my agent, Lauren Spieller, who loved this project first. Thank you to my editor, Courtney Code, for encouraging as many derby shenanigans as possible. Thank you to my illustrator, Sophie Escabasse, for making me cry all those times.

Thank you to the team at Abrams and to everyone who helped this book emerge from a feverish daydream to the real and gorgeous object I am probably clutching at this very moment.

Thank you, Texas Roller Derby Association and Albuquerque Roller Derby, for showing me the ropes/laces of roller derby.

Thank you to Hollins, to Team Triada, to the Epoch5, to BookPeople, to SCBWI, to Pitch Wars, to all my critique partners and writing buddies. Specific thanks to Brian Kennedy, Cory Leonardo, Ash Van Otterloo, Erica Waters, Wendy Heard, Susan Wider, Diana DeBolt, Amanda Rawson Hill, Cindy Baldwin, Jessica Vitalis, Remy Lai, August Smith, and my wonderful friend and mentor Francisco X. Stork.

Eternal gratitude to Jennifer Sigler for cranking the gears behind the curtain and getting me to sit down every day and write the words.

Thank you Cymeon and Jim Watters for letting me use up the printer paper, staples, and pink markers in my early days of making books. Brooke Watters, thank you for being my partner in all things mischievous.

David Rosewater, thank you for pointing down the path to my impossible dream and ordering me to march. You're my favorite.

# ABOUT THE AUTHOR

Kit Rosewater writes books for children. Before she was an author, Kit taught theater to middle school students, which even a world-renowned cat herder once called "a lot of work." Kit has a master's degree in children's literature. She lives in Albuquerque, New Mexico, with her spouse and a border collie who takes up most of the bed. *The Derby Daredevil*s: *Kenzie Kickstarts a Team* is her debut. Catch her online at kitrosewater.com or @kitrosewater.

# ABOUT THE ILLUSTRATOR

Sophie Escabasse is the author-illustrator of the forthcoming graphic novel trilogy The Witches of Brooklyn. She lives in Brooklyn, New York, with her family. Find her online at esofii.com or @esofiii.